Ebenezer Jones

Studies of Sensation and Event

Ebenezer Jones

Studies of Sensation and Event

ISBN/EAN: 9783744763523

Printed in Europe, USA, Canada, Australia, Japan

Cover: Foto ©Andreas Hilbeck / pixelio.de

More available books at **www.hansebooks.com**

STUDIES

OF SENSATION AND EVENT

Studies of Sensation and Event

POEMS

BY

EBENEZER JONES

EDITED PREFACED AND ANNOTATED BY RICHARD HERNE
SHEPHERD WITH MEMORIAL NOTICES OF THE AUTHOR
BY SUMNER JONES AND WILLIAM JAMES LINTON

LONDON
PICKERING AND CO. 196 PICCADILLY
1879

CONTENTS.

STUDIES OF SENSATION AND EVENT :

Studies of Sensation and Event:

Studies of Resemblance and Consent:

PREFACE

BY THE EDITOR.

"THIS remarkable poet," wrote Mr. Dante Rossetti
more than nine years ago of Ebenezer Jones, "affords
nearly the most striking instance of neglected genius
in our modern school of poetry. His poems (the
Studies of Sensation and Event) are full of vivid disorderly power. I was little more than a lad at the
time I first chanced on them, but they struck me
greatly, though I was not blind to their glaring defects,
and even to the ludicrous side of their wilful 'newness ;'
attempting, as they do, to deal recklessly with those
almost inaccessible combinations in nature and feeling
which only intense and oft-renewed effort may perhaps
at last approach. *For all this, these 'Studies' should
be, and one day will be, disinterred* from the heaps of
verse deservedly buried.

"I met him only once in my life, I believe in 1848, at which time he was about thirty, and would hardly talk on any subject but Chartism.

"Some years after meeting Jones, I was much pleased to hear the great poet Robert Browning speak in warm terms of the merit of his work ; and I have understood that Monckton Milnes (Lord Houghton) admired the ' Studies.'*

"The only other recognition of this poet which I have observed is the appearance of a short but admirable lyric by him in the collection called *Nightingale Valley,* edited by William Allingham.

"*It is fully time that attention should be called to this poet's name,* which is a noteworthy one."

Such, in substance, was the warm and generous response of a living man of genius, himself distinguished equally as a poet and as a painter, to a stray question which found its way in the early part of 1870 into that

---

† "He spoke with enthusiasm," writes Mr. Watts, "of the exquisite little poem called 'The Face.' Indeed, there is a lovely poem of his own, with a kindred *motif,* in his 'Poems of Many Years,' beginning

They seem'd to those who saw them meet."

invaluable repository of out-of-the-way information, *Notes and Queries.*

That letter of Mr. D. G. Rossetti's was my first introduction to Ebenezer Jones and to his *Studies of Sensation and Event.* On examining the volume I found it no way disappointed (say rather exceeded) the high expectations thus raised of it, and I determined I would some day, if opportunity served, give fulfilment to Mr. Rossetti's prophecy.

Pressure of more urgent literary work between the years 1873–76—postponed the execution of a scheme which I never ceased to cherish; but when in the summer of last year (1878) there was a lull in my other literary engagements and I was really in search of a subject, it seemed the time had at length come for doing something. About the middle of August, I accordingly issued, as the first of a series of monographs entitled "Forgotten Books worth Remembering," a little brochure giving a brief account of Ebenezer Jones and his volume, and quoting some half-dozen of his most striking and remarkable lyrics. Meagre as, from want of material, the pamphlet necessarily was in all that concerned biographical information, it was nevertheless fortunate enough to do good service in attracting attention to and awakening interest in the subject.

Hardly had it been published a month when the brilliant and graphic series of papers commenced in the *Athenœum*, in which Mr. Theodore Watts told with a picturesque power of writing unrivalled since Mrs. Gaskell's account of the early life of the Brontës, the beautiful and touching story of Ebenezer Jones's early life and struggles, and of the love that knit together himself and his elder brother and sister Sumner and Mary.

These papers, extending through three numbers of the journal in which they appeared,* served the double purpose of familiarising the reading public with a name they had forgotten, or to speak more properly, had never known; and to correct certain mis-statements of fact calculated to give an altogether erroneous idea of Ebenezer Jones's life, mind and character, which had gone abroad with a semblance of

* Sept. 21, Sept. 28, and Oct. 12, 1878.

authority in a letter following Mr. Rossetti's, signed with a name well known in art and literature, and appearing in *Notes and Queries* just a month after his.*

The interest of students and the curiosity of general readers being now everywhere well awakened, it seemed to me that the time had come for making a serious and definitive attempt to resuscitate Ebenezer Jones as a poet. Now, surely, or never! Having sought and obtained the approval and assistance of his nearest surviving relatives and friends (and notably of his brother, Mr. Sumner Jones, of Mr. Horace Harral, and of Mr. W. J. Linton), I accordingly at once devoted myself to the task. Mr. Sumner Jones and Mr. Linton have supplied the eloquent and invaluable memorial notices, from which I do not propose to detain the reader any longer. And Mr. Harral, with the promptest kindness and generosity, entrusted to me for use a mass of his friend's papers—consisting mainly of unpublished poems, rescued as brands from the burning, and containing things as fine as any in his published book.

* *Notes and Queries*, March 5, 1870.

Should the present volume meet with a reasonable amount of acceptance, I propose to publish a second in the autumn, containing a selection from these, together with a reprint of the pamphlet on the Land Monopoly, some other prose pieces, and perhaps a few letters. This second volume will also contain a very remarkable photographic portrait of the author, executed by two artist friends of his, of which the negative has fortunately been preserved. I shall reserve till then also what I have to say myself respecting Ebenezer Jones's life and work and his place among the poets of his age. I have given way in this volume to those who have a prior and a better right to speak about him; and it has already exceeded its intended limits.

RICHARD HERNE SHEPHERD.

CHELSEA, *May,* 1879.

EBENEZER JONES:

IN MEMORIAM.

UNDER date 8th January 1870, inquiry was made
in "Notes and Queries," No. 106, over the signature
of F. Gledstanes-Waugh, for "particulars of the life"
of EBENEŻER JONES, "the above-named Chartist"—
as he is incorrectly styled — whose Poems entitled
" Studies of Sensation and Event," published in 1843,
and now termed "a very striking book," have long
been out of print.

EBENEZER JONES was my younger brother, and
I wish to correct some mis-statements made in
"Notes and Queries," in reply to the above inquiry, and also to supply some of the particulars
requested—the former in order that I may be faithful
to his memory, around which, until 1870, there had
been unbroken silence since his death; the latter with
reference mainly to the conditions under which the

c

book referred to was produced, since with a purposed reticence very rare in young writers similarly circumstanced, he gave no hint prefatorily or textually of those conditions. Yet they possess that interest which must always be inseparable from the relation of the early struggles of genius. And they will throw light upon the character and texture of poems, the unfulfilled promise of which cannot be fairly estimated unless the conditions incident to their production are taken into account.

Long before the inquiry above referred to came to my knowledge, subsequent numbers (110–114) of " Notes and Queries "* show that both Mr. D. G. Rossetti and Mr. W. B. Scott had furnished, separately, some account of Eben Jones, based on such slight knowledge of him as those writers possessed.

There are inaccuracies in both accounts—due doubtless to lapse of time and hearsay information.

These, however, weigh nothing against the generous and touching testimony borne by Mr. Rossetti to the vitality of the first productions of a young poet who long before his death, in 1860, had reason to believe that his work, aspersed and neglected as it was, had become finally forgotten.

Mr. Scott alludes to my brother as a " remarkable

* " Notes and Queries," 4th S., v. 154, 264 (February 5 and March 5, 1870).

man"—which he was, quite apart from his poetry—
and states that the term "Chartist" had been gratui-
tously applied to him.   This I confirm, and I thank
Mr. Scott for that prompt correction. It may be proper
to add, that the writer of the "Studies" would not
have considered the term one of reproach; but he
neither avowed himself a Chartist, nor would he have
recognised the fitness of that label for his political
opinions, which went deeper than Chartism, and had
a much wider horizon.   There is no allusion whatever
to Chartists in his book, by which alone he can be
remembered; and to term him a "Chartist poet" is
therefore clearly a mistake which ought to be, and
now is, corrected.

Critical remarks by mature poets on the first-fruits
of a young author, produced under such circumstances
as those to be described, I will pass over. I stood too
near to him during the whole of his life, and my
memory of him now is too quick with affection, to
enable me to discuss his poems critically, even were I
otherwise qualified to do so.

It may be observed, however, in passing, that
poems stated by Mr. W. B. Scott to be the product of
a "poetic faculty" which "was wholly impulsive,"
have seemed to others fraught with evidence of an eager
mind less moved by mere poetic impulse than intent
upon poetic thinking, and often recoiling upon itself

c 2

in order to ascertain and test the authenticity of its emotions. Be this as it may, I know that his aim was to be, in his own words, a "poetical thinker," and an "Ode to Thought"* is the first written poem in the volume.

Some minor inaccuracies require notice. He wrote no "pamphlet on the Currency" after he forsook his true sphere, Poetry. He wrote, however, and published two pamphlets. One, I think, was entitled "The Condition of England Question ;" but of that I can now find no trace. The other was entitled "The Land Monopoly, the suffering and demoralization caused by it, and the justice and expediency of its abolition." This was published in 1849,† and is before me as I write. Here he expressly denounces Communism in a very striking passage, but there is no allusion even here to Chartism, though the preceding year, 1848, was the Chartist year, and the throne-shaking year for Europe, when many older men than Eben Jones—then aged twenty-eight—were, for a time, fairly carried off their feet.

He had from boyhood a decided and not a mere theoretical leaning to a Republican form of Government, but his philosophical tolerance of opinions opposed to his own is shown in a Sonnet, "Opinion's

* See pp. 58–61.

† By Charles Fox, Paternoster-row, pp. 28 (including title).

Change," where he counsels the "beardless statesman," and adds :—

> " But learn'd to think, he sees that men in a King
>   Find much they need,—a thing to which must bow
> Masters as low as serfs ; a man whose brow
> Is highest in the State, and yet must spring
>   Smiles to their smiles—and so he lets enjoy
> Mankind its many Kings, as a child its toy."*

Caroline Atherstone — to whom he was so
lamentably allied in marriage in 1844—was not a
daughter, but a niece, of the late Edwin Atherstone.
Not one line in his book has that reference to her
which is clearly implied by the context of Mr. Scott's
remark :—"Ebenezer's day of poetry was his day of
love." The book was published before they ever met,
and much of it was written while love was yet confined
to the circle of home. Those poems to which the
remark does apply were inspired by one who was
lost to him by change and estrangement, and who not
long after was claimed by death.

All this happened to him before he published. It
will sufficiently indicate what is here meant, to state
that the poems "Repose in Love," "Happy Sadness,"
"Dismounting a Mistress," in contrast with "The
Face," "Prayer to a Fickle Mistress," with its
mournful burden, "Once say you are sad for me,"
together with still more revealing passages in "A

* Page 110.

Crisis," are pages torn from life, and which tell a story of their own.

But beyond what he has himself so disclosed, that story—those "particulars" of his life—must for ever remain untold.

There is no foundation for the statement that "interest on the author's behalf" was at any time shown in any quarter; nor, since the phrase clearly implies material interest, is there, on that score, any room for regret. For with that utter independence of spirit which was the very breath of life to my brother, and was even dearer to him than song, he not only never looked for this, but held himself studiously aloof from eliciting it. On the other hand, the nobler "interest" involved in recognition of him as an independent poet—if not of achievement, then of promise—he did most ardently desire, and *that* he strove manfully to obtain.

But that, also, as shown by the fate of his poems, was denied to him during his life. And not merely by the so-called critics of the day, but by some in an inner circle, to whom, with the mingled faith and humility of true genius, he made, or rather permitted to be made, through the writer of this sketch, to whom they were personally known, a final but vain appeal.

Needful corrections thus disposed of, I will now

endeavour to give, in outline, some of the desired particulars of my dear brother's life—a life bare of external incident, but thronged at the outset with passions and with kindling aspirations, which, with rare force of will, he schooled into patience on a path of narrow and to him utterly alien toil.

His struggle for outlet was aided only by the power he felt within him, and when that struggle resulted in aspersion of his motives and his work, that also, after the one appeal for fair play to which I have referred, was borne in silence to the end.

Silence was his sole answer to his anonymous accusers. And since he took that silence with him to the grave to deepen there, it seemed to me that what he disdained to do, it would be wrong for me to attempt.

But, with others of his kindred, I am forced to see that while the silence has been broken by generous tribute to his memory, there is in one of the notices above referred to, allusion to that old painful charge of "impure motive," not as wandering out obscurely from the journalism of his day, but now for the first time stamped with the sanction of the honoured name of Thomas Hood. Perhaps no other name could give equal currency to that charge ; could so convince ordinary readers—seeing the notice in question, but not the book, nor even passages from it—that such censure of a young poet by an elder one deemed so humane, so charitable, must have been merited indeed.

Nevertheless, the charge is one which no just and competent critic can substantiate from the book. I disclaim resentful feeling in regard to the revival of this painful charge, thus endorsed. Rather I reflect that if the fact—for fact it is—that the book fell under the *private* ban of Hood, had (why, I know not) to be *publicly* stated twenty-seven years afterwards, and in context with the words that my brother was "rendered miserable," as though he admitted the charge ; then it is better so now than hereafter—now, while a brother lives who would plead with Detraction itself to spare his name.

The one fact in the matter is what I here set down as fact. All the rest is apocryphal. Hood never sent for my brother. My brother never went to, nor even saw Hood. Hood did not even write to my brother; his letter was addressed to myself, who had taken the book to him with my brother's consent, and though it was a very severe, and even 'savage' letter, it was my brother, who was a most just man, who pointed out to me in the midst of my vexation at all this, that Hood had evidently written conscientiously, and from a sense of duty, and so he undoubtedly had. Then sitting down in my presence, he penned at once a brief but very courteous note in

reply, which was merely to the effect that he regretted
to receive such an expression of opinion from one
he honoured so much, but regretted still more the
mistake that he now perceived had been made in
placing the book before him. That was all. I saw
the note.

It was the public attacks, such as that in the *Literary
Gazette,** that troubled my brother. He despised them,
never noticed them ; but he saw clearly that they involved the failure of his book, and with that of his
darling hope that he might obtain some better em-
ployment, with more margin of leisure than was
possible where he was. Hood's *private* censure, coming
after the public hurt was inflicted, could not and
did not affect matters, but left them where they
were. How could that render any rational person
"miserable?" On the contrary, there was room for
congratulation that Hood, who it was hoped would
review the book in his *own* Magazine, had *not* openly
done *that*, which would have made matters worse ;
and so we both felt before we separated that
evening.

Nine years have passed since Mr. Scott wrote his
notice. What I have here written is my refutation of
the charge, and my contradiction of the alleged facts ;

* December 23, 1843.

and imperative to me that I should speak is the voice
that seems to issue from my brother's grave.

> " I shall remember I was pure ;
>   Fearlessly loving, ever, the whole,"*

was his utterance of himself who sleeps there.

I remember too.—I remember him back to the days
of his childhood, and almost infancy, before we took
our first hand-in-hand slide together ; remember smile,
tone, gesture, that marked him out from others in his
daring days of boyhood ; and how in early manhood,
when he began to think, I loved to track across his
mobile features the unworded thought ; and I *know*
that whatever there may seem to be too pronounced,
or too warmly sportive, in some of his pages, it is false
to accuse him of deliberately writing with " impure
motive," for that never stained his mind.

His own words above-quoted compass much that I
would say.   " Fearlessly loving ever the whole," *was*
the ideal life he sought to live, was the instinct of his
nature, and was the only way for one who was born
to side with the noble Few, ever striving to be brave
enough for Truth.   It was also the way to incur for
early endeavour to embody love of " the whole " in
artistic form, while the conception was as yet im-
mature, the easy scoff of little men, and misconception

* *Remembrance of Feelings,* p. 56.

even by good men, whose feebler passions and less vivid insight lead them consciously, or unconsciously, to elect only to love a part.

Mr. Rossetti expressed an opinion that my brother's forgotten poems would "one day be disinterred." Certain it is, although unknown to Mr. Rossetti when he so wrote, that Eben Jones did not wish to be forgotten, to be quite "left out of the story," since after seventeen all but silent years as regards poetry (1843–1860, when he died) a "Winter Hymn to the Snow," and a few other simple verses, written during his last illness, and hitherto unpublished, were held forth in his dying hand.

And since a stranger laying down his solitary book felt prompted to ask, at large, for some knowledge of the life of him who wrote it, it is natural to conclude that others hereafter may echo the wish that something at least could be known of the fate of one who in his early youth so stamped his own fervid mind upon his work.

To respond to that wish—while as my own main object seeking to vindicate his memory from reproach—will be my aim in the outline I now propose to give.

EBENEZER JONES was the third child and the second son of Robert Jones, a gentleman of Welsh descent, by his second marriage with Hannah Sumner,* the youngest daughter of Richard Sumner, head of a family long settled in Essex, and in that county—especially in the churchyard of Hadleigh, a village well-known for the massive ruins of an old Castle in the vicinity—family vaults of the Sumners will be found.

Not intending to write a word of family history, but simply to delineate as accurately as can be done in outline, one vivid and intensely individual life born into that family, I pass on at once to state that Eben Jones was born in Canonbury-square, Islington, on the 20th of January 1820.

That suburb of London, sixty years ago, still had green spaces around it which have long disappeared. Near the house in which Eben was born, on the verge of extensive fields, stood all that remained of the ancient Manor-house of Canonbury, and that well-known brick tower is still standing. An old pond under the shadow of that tower has, I believe, long been filled up; but my earliest clear remembrance of

* There were six children by this marriage, three sons and three daughters :—Mary, born 10th October 1816, died 14th December 1838 ; Sumner, born 22nd April 1818 ; EBENEZER, born 20th January 1820 ; David Robert, born 1st May 1822 ; Selina, born 9th October 1824, died 1862 ; and Hannah (the heroine of Ebenezer's beautiful poem of *The Hand*), born 15th April, 1827, died 1st February 1879.—ED.

Ebby (always his household name) was holding hands with him for a slide on the frozen surface of that pond when he was about four years old.

His parents were in competent circumstances, and all the surroundings of his childhood and early boyhood were so far favourable. But—belonging as they did, with all their immediate connexions, to a very strict sect of Calvinist dissenters—their chief aim as regarded the education of their children was sedulously to train them on a narrow path, through what was termed the "wilderness of this world," from any genuine knowledge of which they were thus excluded until precipitated into it early in life—and at a most grievous disadvantage, in consequence of such bringing up—by the force of events.

The young mind of my brother, "finely touched" from childhood, but wholly unappreciated by all who could influence his future career in life, was dieted at home (we were a bookish family) alternately on books in which "useful knowledge" was framed in a setting of religious "tags"—books of solid doctrinal divinity, and, worst of all, books of over-wrought "spiritual" experience and hysterical evangelism, such as I hope are not published now; while the Bible, and a compilation of short Questions and long Answers (we wished it had been the other way), dreaded by us, and called the "Assembly's Catechism," were in constant use to fill up all gaps. Dr. Watts and Kirke White were permitted on our Parnassus; but Shakespeare and even Milton were kept in rigorous quarantine. Of Byron we had a mysterious notion, gathered from hearing our elders now and then speak of him shudderingly, as of some Satanic spirit who had been permitted visibly to stalk abroad. Of Shelley we had never heard. Card-playing and dancing were denounced, and those who indulged in them were looked upon as doomed.

Schools—private schools—were selected less for educational advantages than because they were conducted by ministers of the same iron Calvinist creed, the tenets of which were a terror to us in our youth. All this was otherwise carried out with pious intention, aided by flagellation, to an extreme at which I do but hint here, but which, when the inevitable day of revolt arrived, resulted in the opposite extreme; and this is mentioned here because the result of such collision of extremes may, I think, be traced in some of my brother's poems.

In a first book of verse it would indeed have been specific, and marked, save for his very studious habits of self-culture, so far as he had opportunity—which, as will be seen, was not far—after school-days had elapsed.

In connexion with his school-life, one little incident ought to be recorded before I pass on, because it first singled him out from all around him—myself included—and disclosed, as it has always seemed to me, even in the child, that force of passion which marks the poems of the man.

"You shall not!" was his bold and defiant utterance of himself, thus publicly uttered in my hearing and ineffaceably stamped upon my memory, before he can have been nine years old.

We were together at a well-known boarding-school of that day (1828), situated at the foot of Highgate Hill, and presided over by a dissenting minister, the Rev. John Bickerdike, whose peculiar nasal feature had earned for him among us boys the appellation of "Snipe." It was a theme of frequent discussion among us whether the worthy man had ever found that out—which some of us believed and some not.

We were together, though not on the same form; and on a hot summer afternoon, with about fifty other boys, were listlessly conning our tasks in a large school-room built out from the house, which made cover for us to play under when it was wet. Up the ladder-like stairs from the play-ground a lurcher dog had strayed into the school-room, panting with the heat, his tongue lolling out with thirst. The choleric usher who presided, and was detested by us for his tyranny, seeing this, advanced down the room. Enraged at our attention being distracted from our tasks, he dragged the dog to the top of the stairs, and there lifted him bodily up with the evident intention—and we had known him do similar things—of hurling the poor creature to the bottom.

"You shall not!" rang through the room, as little Ebby, so exclaiming at the top of his voice, rushed with kindling face to the spot from among all the boys—some of them twice his age.

But even while the words passed his lips, the heavy fall was heard, and the sound seemed to travel through his listening form and face, as, with a strange look of anguish in one so young, he stood still, threw up his arms, and burst out into an uncontrollable passion of tears.

With a coarse laugh at this, the usher led him back by his ear to the form ; and there he sat, long after his sobbing had subsided, like one dazed and stunned.

That little incident stands out from all others of that time, and those words, " You shall not !" ring in my memory.

Often, in after years, a somewhat similar look would come into his face, when his thought, even on a summer ramble, such as he has described in his poem, "Inactivity,"* took him into that region which he

* pp. 86-91.

lived to haunt so much, and which the Germans have named " *world-sorrow.*"

Finding a fragment of some long-ago record made of some such summer Sunday ramble when (1839–40–1) I was his companion, as I would often be, it is here inserted, because it depicts him from life as he then was, in his musing mood, on a day of the "High Summer" he so delighted in, and is better than description from memory, even when she holds the mirror in which, closing my eyes, I see his that were so keen and thrillingly beautiful; and it does not seem to be remembrance, but actual re-appearance then, for a moment—but he cannot stay.

> " About him humm'd the labouring bee ;
>   The squirrel ran up the tall tree ;
>   Faint cuckoo-calls came drowsed with heat ;
>   Larks dropp'd and nestled near his feet ;
>   And thrice a young Delight he knew
>   Flew round him, and before him flew,
>   With 'sweet, sweet, sweet—and all for you.'
>   He sat upon a stile apart,
>   The world's convulsion in his heart ;
>   But in his fix'd space-searching eye,
>   Conquest—far off, eternally."

At other times, amid such scenes, he would be gay and happy and full of laughter, such laughter as he has himself described as—

> " the gentle lift
> Of gently joy-breezed life."*

* *The Naked Thinker* (p. 4).

d

And yet those were the days when, as will presently be seen, we were working together twelve hours daily at the same city desk, and he was wringing from his nights and his Sundays the time both to live his life and to write his poems.

I return for a moment to school-days.

The incident above related was followed by no apparent change in him, excepting that he would now occasionally break off from sport, and climb with some book in play-hours up into the poplar trees that bordered the play-ground fence, to read and peer about alone.

In one of his poems are the lines :—

> " From sunsets flushing heaven with sudden crimson
>   To the moth's wing that spots the poplar leaf ;"*—

which I told him had that 'habitat' in his memory, and he smiled.

Of his really juvenile verse one fragment remains on a time-stained page which has accidentally escaped destruction, and for the sake of the child-like simplicity of the lines, and a certain consciousness which they evince of what he even then felt stirring within him, I transcribe them here. They denote his favourite habit, above alluded to, of climbing into trees, with the life of which he had intense sympathy. He was a boy of about fourteen, home for the holidays, when this was written, as shown by a deceased sister's

---

* *A Development of Idiotcy* (p. 71).

papers among which it was found, and is here unen-titled, as on the page :—

> " See, sister, yonder is the bank
>   Where the dragon-flies did play;
> How often have I broke the rank
>   Of school-fellows and stole away
> To climb that very beechen tree,
>   To con some old romantic story
> Of Jewish maid or Alice Lee—
>   Of knightly love and feudal glory.
>
> While the stately sun was going
>   Like a hero to his bride,
> On my leafy study throwing
>   His parting glance of pride.
> Then came to me the joys, the fears—
>   The lofty hopes of poetry,
> And brightly shone my future years,
>   I stood and gazed exultingly.
>
> And sometimes 'neath my lofty bower
>   A beauteous girl would wander by—
> I knew not then that wealth was power,
>   That love from poverty would fly :
> With ardent and devoted pride
>   I read in her sky-watching eyes
> Genius might win a lovely bride,
>   And vow'd to gain the prize."

Comparison of these lines with " The Kings of Gold," or the "Ode to Thought," which appeared in magazines about four years after, will show the progress made in that time ; but some tender streak of light that comes before the dawn seems to me discernible even here ; and the boy in his "leafy study," on whom the sun threw "his parting glance of pride," might, had the world dealt better with him, or dealt even with common fairness, have made himself a memorable man.

I now pass on to the time when a long illness of the head of the family resulted disastrously, and all hope of the training of the sons for professional pursuit was at an end.

This change in his prospects, although it became clear that he would soon have to stand forth in the market-place of the world, caused him no immediate despondency. For with the falling away of ministers and their allies (for whom our father's house had been quite an unctuously-esteemed rendezvous) to other quarters where high Calvinism could still be solidly supported by Consols, and the altar for family worship flanked by the lavish hospitality such persons prized, there came an irruption of new ideas which bore down, absolutely and for ever, and as with a cataract of jubilation, all the old restraint.

Now was the veritable awaking of my brother's mind ! I do not so much recall that time, as see it return, and re-enact itself vividly before me as I write.

There was in him nothing whatever of that vacillating purblind conflict curiously called "spiritual," which weaker minds so dealt with have often cruelly to undergo. He felt intuitively that the grim tenets which had manacled his childhood, had been inherited by both parents through lives of their progenitors, and that it was owing to the parents being themselves over-shadowed by dark beliefs that the children had been screened from light. Irreparable was the loss (he always felt that) that the bright and wide-believing eye of childhood had not been permitted to see fairly unrolled the great panorama of life, and the true world of men and women and their work.

But from the dark corner where he had been forced to crouch beneath a Moloch of man's invention, he boldly emerged, and poetry and religion became one with him—contemplating a Presence he could now both adore and love,

> "unto whom now I offer
> Rapt adoration which no priestly scoffer
> Of thee and thy dear love may hope to know,"

as he wrote in perished boy-verse of that time.

In the same spirit he will be found in the "Studies" renouncing, yet religiously renouncing, the "worship of terror-wrenched thanks."

> "How vast must be thy blessedness, aye sphering
> Happy bright planets from the galaxy,
> Thereon inhoming us intelligents !
> Lover that knows no weariness !
>
> *   *   *   *
>
> "Time sounds of life which scare us listening here,
> Shaking our faith with their unanswer'd plainings,

> Play sweetly unto thine eternal mind
> The discords of one deepening harmony !"*

He has been charged with " profanity," (I use the word in its conventional meaning), but the charge was false on the evidence of his book.   The above passage with others, such as the simple lines at the close of " Two Sufferers," commencing " Children of earth ! believe,"† are sufficient disproof of this.

It is true as stated (*Notes and Queries*, No. 110) that "vivid " but " disorderly" power is stamped on some of his poems, written during the " storm and stress" of after years.   But it is also true, and now known only to me (and to me incommunicably) that in the fair beginning, before that happened to him which seemed to take for him the sun out of the sky and leave all blackness, and the verdure from the earth and leave all barrenness—he sought to

> " Leap with his passionate reason down the depths,
> Tempestuously toss'd, of human nature,
> Seeking the masked demons that invoke
> Suffering and wrong ;"‡

only that he might in the end be enabled more firmly, the storm of passion over and the knowledge gained, to approach his favourite idea of creative art in song, which was that of " harmonizing elements."

---

* *Egremond* (p. 15 of the original edition of the *Studies*).
† p. 46.   ‡ *Egremond* (*ubi suprà*, p. 12).

His mind was now fairly aroused, and books hitherto proscribed, and which we had been taught to consider of a "worldly" character and worse, could no longer be suppressed.

Carlyle's "French Revolution" was lent to him, not very long after its publication; and later on "Sartor Resartus" was read, and "burned within him." A little thick duodecimo edition of Shelley's Poems was also obtained, and this had afterwards a magical effect upon him. But it was at first Carlyle's famous History that became among us a "Sensation and Event."

Whole passages from Carlyle were got by heart among us, and recited—one from his "Sartor Resartus," commencing "Two men I honour, and no third," was an especial favourite. Passing each other on the stairs, however hurriedly, my brother—our elder sister shaking her curls with joy and beaming smiles upon us—and the writer of this sketch, would chant forth those words, "Two men I honour, and no third," in a swift rejoicing way, in token of our freedom—our new-found creed—and as the vanguard of the new ideas which were now rapidly expanding in my brother's mind.

More than forty years, with all their joys, sorrows and illusions have since rolled away; yet still as I write, a wave of sound from that far past seems travelling on, freighted with his resonant voice, toning out the words of that passage :—

" Hardly-entreated brother ! For us was thy back so bent, for us were thy straight limbs and fingers so deformed : thou wert our conscript, on whom the lot fell, and fighting our battles wert so marred."*

Other books followed in rapid succession, and he now betook himself vigorously to composition both in prose and verse, but chiefly prose. Among lost exercises of this time I specially remember the following :—"My relations to the Universe in so far as I seem to have present discernment of them ;" written as a sort of mental seed-plot in which to sow his newly-acquired ideas and thoughts ; " On the nature and office of Poetry," written to the sub_ject as given to be read before an Association he had joined for a time. With this he took great pains, sending it in with his favourite motto "*Homo sum,*" &c., and it was a remarkable Essay, preserved for many years by himself, who destroyed so much, and I deplore that it was not finally preserved.

There were also Songs of which I can recall no echo, and many series of Sonnets ; a poem too on " Slavery under the American Republic," which I regret he excluded from his book.

> " Land of the West ! how great thy shame
>   Amid immortal graves,
> Within the Holy Place of fame,
>   To shackle slaves."

* *Sartor Resartus*, Book iii. chap. 4, § Helotage.

are lines in it which cling to memory, and an invocation to the spirit of Washington in the same poem, was for a youth of seventeen nobly penned.

These metrical compositions, written before he had ever thought of publication, he would give to the sister I have mentioned, a gifted girl of whom he was proudly fond, striving with tender art to give her back some of her own cherished ideas set in the wider light of his now kindling mind.

She, not destined long to survive the family troubles, died at the age of twenty-two. After her first taste of the new ideas with her brothers, the wings of her mind were folded up again within the limits of sheltered belief, all her own impassioned feeling for truth and beauty passing into unwavering and even ecstatic faith under her chosen

> " Leader of faithful souls and guide
> Of those who travel to the sky "—

and so she passed into her rest.

In after years some verses appeared in a periodical commencing :—

> " Twice three years in this tomb she hath lain,
> Speak low, speak low ;"—

which he wrote on revisiting this sister's grave. Often would he recur to the days when on a Sunday evening, he would close his books and escort her to the chapel of her choice, strolling himself through lanes and fields.

now built over, but where then the nightingale sang, until it was time to guard her home again ; and often have I heard him, when dwelling upon her gentle memory, rejoice that he had been able to read section xxxiii. of the Laureate's "In Memoriam" without remorse.

In the year 1837 Eben was placed out in business, in the world of which he had been allowed to know little or nothing. He was still but seventeen. With an instinctive shudder on the verge of traffic, he endeavoured rather to remain as junior usher in his last school. But this was overruled, and a house of business in the City was selected, where began that exacting round of office labour, which alas ! for him was only to cease with life.

Here knowledge and remembrance merge into experience, since I worked with him in the same office for six years (1837–43), when my steps were diverted into another path. Our hours of business were twelve daily, from 8 a.m. to 8 p.m., exclusive of getting to and from the premises. They were severe even for those days, nor had the great boon of the Saturday half-holiday then been thought of.

The remainder of the family had gone to settle in Wales, on the wreck of the family fortunes ; and we two were left stranded alone in London, and at first especially, the long day's sedentary work done, we would reach our lodgings at night exhausted.

Plea made for a margin of time for health—for he was still but a growing boy—or for self-culture, was met by the rejoinder, that self-culture led to pride of intellect, which (in their odious jargon) was " one of Satan's peculiar snares." This language was actually held by men—our employers—who though conducting a wholesale business, in which they amassed large fortunes, stooped, as did others like them, to the lowest tricks of retail trade.

Thus, save that his young genius could not be slain, was Mammon left to finish what the bigots had begun.

Well was it that after the inner world of home, with its cramped notions and iron creed, and the outer world of schools which had taught nothing well, there had been that interposition of new ideas which he had grasped so eagerly.

In this case the help was great—the safeguard was immense. For " lion-like passions " were now commencing to awake in him ; they were only lashed by toil, and were tameless save by thought.

The howl of the world had aroused him, as few young men born into the middle class of society are roused amid the smooth compromises of social life to-day. Among others I could point to in the *"Studies,"* pages 153–154, commencing " Dire is the woe,"*—are

* *Ways of Regard.*

passages of poetical autobiography as veritable as were ever penned.

But such words as " Courage ! and forward young brother ! " breathing into his soul from Mr. Carlyle's writings, cheered and sustained him as with a hand which he could grasp. The poet of the " Ode to Liberty," from his station in the heaven of Fame, seemed also to his young enthusiasm to bend over him with a smile. Shelley was much with him at this time : he made allusion to Shelley even when writing argumentatively to M. Considerant,* on his plan for the " Conciliation of Society by the Organization of Labour," printed in 1839, in the " New Moral World " of Robert Owen, to which he contributed, and whose disciple he became for a time. But the doctrine that

---

* " Who wrote the *Revolt of Islam ?* Not Shelley ! 'Tis the mighty utterance of a society whose eyes have just opened to the glory of truth, and she made him her priest. He was but the lute ; she the power of music—he was but the prophet ; she was the God."—This letter to M. Considerant also appeared in the first number of *The Promethean, or Communitarian Apostle, a Monthly Magazine,* edited by Goodwyn Barmby, January 1842. Mr. Goodwyn Barmby writes to me (from Westgate Parsonage, Wakefield, 22nd March 1879) — " Eben and myself were very good friends, and he was a noble and manly fellow. . . I have looked over my " Promethean " Magazine, in which Eben Jones wrote two politico-economical articles"—[the other being " Arguments for and against Private Property"], but no verses, and in which are some beautiful verses by Sumner Jones."—ED.

circumstance is the sole formative of " character " had small charm for one who was resolved to overcome circumstance, and hoped to force himself, unaided, out of his obscurity.

His " Song of the Gold-Getters,"* with its chorus, " Lie ! let us lie, make the lies fit," has been censured as cynical. Yet, seeing what was round him, he did but so, in biting words, translate the very gospel of the men he was now so closely connected with, and of hosts of their competitors.

Their name is legion. They are men who, in place of deploring, as do some in business, the evils inseparable from excessive competition, intensify them all by their own sinister dealings. They are men who relish most of all their " gold-getting," just those very base accretions of profit that stick between successful lies, and they are men—I know them to the core— whose frankest smile signs furtive meaning, and whose shake of the hand is fraud.

Not until his first year in the counting-house was nearly over did he rally and break through his gloom. The earliest of the poems preserved in his book is the " Ode to Thought," sent at a venture to Tait's Magazine, and inserted in September 1838.

In that poem, written under the circumstances now described, he invokes the " Spirits of Thought " to his

* pp. 94-96.

aid. He utters no lament, he indicates nothing of his position among men, nor is there earthly love nor thirst for personal fame ; but the young poet seeks in thought communion with the Source of Thought, and a poem in some respects distinct from any other in the volume, closes with the prayer :—

" Fill me with strength to bear and power to tell
    The wonders gathering round, that man may love me well."*

Such was his young ambition. And the power was vouchsafed to him, though not to be matured on earth.

Though it be but for "trivial fond record," I would fain relax here from bare outline, since it will somewhat relieve what has to follow, and to linger here a little is to look at the breaking light.

It was the hand now holding the pen that brought to him the magazine in which the poem appeared, as soon as it could be procured ; and I still see him as he dived from his desk in the counting-house down to the warehouse basement with this, his first printed poem that he cared about—returning soon, with a happy smile. Writing on an office slip, "I feel as if I should do now," he passed it to where I sat.

That night, walking to our common lodging in the Old Kent Road, he confided to me, for the first time, his hope that he would yet, one day,

---

* pp. 61. The original version in *Tait* differs, however, in the lines above quoted.—ED.

emancipate himself by his pen from City thraldom,
and not himself alone. But there was "Fool,"
our faithful dog (though when was dog not faithful ?), whom we had so named after the Fool in
"King Lear," and who was prized by us both as a
relic of home. He must have his nightly scamper,
somehow. "Would you see to that sometimes while
I write ? " "Would you mind that ? " So he talked
whose speech did but forerun his act—for from that
time forth, after working in the City all day, he set
himself to bend night to his fixed resolve, and com-
pleted, during the next four years, a series of poems
of which the "Studies" are but a selection.

And during those years—that happening to him
which has been hinted at in the commencement of this
sketch—the inspiration of woman's love failed him ;
but he did not fail, though now he had to be strong
with lonely strength ; not that strength of silent
endurance only which fixed his latter life, but as he
wrote at this period dauntless and " strong to dare."*
And he wrestled in thought to "rend life's seemings,
and drag out the things that are,"† turning upon the
world which he felt he now knew, with the cry—

> "I hurl detecting scorn
> At life's old harlot zone,
> I crush her masks for centuries worn,
> I strip her on her throne.‡"

* *The Suicide* (p. 107).　　† *The Naked Thinker* (p.8).
‡ *Ibid*, p. 7.

while shaking around him as it were the spear of a young Ishmael of Song—and yet those years, because as a poet he still had hope for his ally, were the happiest years my noble-hearted brother was ever destined to know.

The reception given to his volume is stated in the notices which have called for this sketch. Specimens of the perverse and lying criticism of that day may be found in the *Literary Gazette*, and other journals. And I have stated what was the result of private appeal to elder bards.

He felt that it was enough. As he himself wrote—

> " As some full cloud foregoes his native country
> Of sublime hills, where bask'd he near to heaven,
> And descends gently on his shadowy wings
> Through the hot sunshine to refresh all creatures ;
> So came he to the world ;—as the same cloud
> Might slowly wend back to his Alpine home,
> Unwatering the plain ;—so left he men
> Who knew not of their loss.*"

I have now given some account of the circumstances under which these poems were put forth, from the seething world of Mincing-lane, by a young poet-student who commenced to work there for his bread some forty years ago.

* *A Development of Idiotcy* (p. 71).

Dr. Johnson, whose sturdy definition of the word "patron," was greatly relished by the author of the "Studies", observes in his Life of Butler, that "when any work has been viewed and admired, the first question of intelligent curiosity is, how was it performed?" This I have endeavoured to answer in my sketch; and I think even those who may have little or no regard for endeavour taking any direction save that of material success, must yet admire the energy, the perseverance, and the indomitable will my brother displayed.

Many young literary adventurers, especially in poetry, circumstanced as he was, cannot refrain from giving expression to sympathy-begetting hints of their surroundings. It was not so with Eben Jones. Strong in his belief that the poet should be the outcome of the man—never the man merged in the poet, his book *is* the outcome of a strong silent struggle to gain vantage-ground for future work—with which at that time of his life he teemed,—by proof that he was a poet, that master-passion covering another cherished aim, which was to escape from traffic and leave no trace of having been engaged in it behind. In his latter years he never alluded to the "Studies" in conversing with me, save on one occasion when taking the book up only to lay it down again, he remarked that there was nothing in it to track him by, which is true, and that no one could say he had made any "bid for support." He seemed pleased to think of that—greatly pleased.

This was in his parlour in Paultons-square,* where I used to visit him, and after tea he would ask to blow the candles out for a talk in the dark, which he liked when we two were alone. His admiration of the poetical work of Mr. Browning (whom he never met) was intense; and "The Lost Leader," which was after his own heart, was perhaps his favourite poem. He would recur to the days so long gone by when he was wont to thrust "Pippa Passes," as it first appeared (1841) in the thin yellow covers,† into the breast-pocket of his coat, and sally forth for a ramble in the country. "Pippa Passes" was a special favourite. At this time (1858) I now and then brought him little commissions from the city, for a kind of writing at which he was an expert, and that could be done at home. On one occasion, being off my guard, and remarking that this was "sad work for a poet,"—he looked up at me with the thrilling light which to the

* No. 17: he afterwards removed to No. 26: letters of his now lie before me dated from both houses.—ED.

† As No. 1 of the series of *Bells and Pomegranates*, issued in numbers.—ED.

last would come into his eyes, and repeated very gently the closing words of "Pippa Passes"—

> "All service is the same with God,—
> Whose puppets, best and worst,
> Are we—"

and the sweet patience of his smile rebuked my restless thought.

The account I am rendering of my brother, while a faithful, is necessarily a subdued account. The surrounding conditions can be shown; but how depict the eager spirit who soared above those conditions as he revealed himself to me, during those special years of his fore-shortened life? I can and do recall his bright and airy manner, when with elastic step, in the trying round of office-work bearing more heavily (as he knew) on the brother of feebler fibre, he would come across to my desk, press my hand, and whisper, "This is but for a time." But to attempt what is termed "graphic and life-like delineation" of the individuality of his nature, as it fluctuated into so many different moods, transparent through all, and taking tone and colour from a myriad fleeting things,—that would not only be vain, but it would be wrong.

The reader of this sketch, having also the poems in his hand, must be content to learn from me, who have absolute knowledge of it, that the tide of passionate strength in certain pages flowed into them direct from the life of the writer. As his poems are so was he in speech and act; impetuous, yet inflexible, imaginative yet incisive, now with tender and even child-like simplicity, pleading against "slander of my beautiful world,"* now carolling a "Song to a Rose,"† now picturing a leader of revolt (such as he could himself have been), in lines of startling force‡—and anon telling us in a little poem that begins like the first droppings of a shower, how he loves "Rain."§

The reception of his poems was matter of genuine surprise as well as disappointment to my brother. Living as he did quite apart from cliques of writers for the press, and without one literary friend, he ingenuously believed that although, as he had written, "The world is war "‖—he would encounter honest warfare in the literary sphere.

He was prepared to profit by any fair severity of criticism. But seeing passages from his book studiously garbled and wrenched from their context, to convey a false impression of the whole, forced him to hear the "Lie, let us lie," chorus of his world of traffic echoed in an arena where he had thought that a "free lance" would at least meet fair attack. Until thus disillusioned he had indeed fondly imagined that there was a brotherhood in Art.

* *Life* (p. 106 of original edition.) † pp. 101-102.
‡ *Ways of Regard* (p. 102). § pp. 132-133.
‖ *Song of the Gold-getters* (p. 96).

It is right to record on the other hand that he received from several literati, personally unknown to him, to whom he had sent presentation copies of his book, (simply "with the Author's compliments") kind letters in return.

These he would show to me—and I remember one which was very gratifying to him from Mr. Procter (Barry Cornwall), and another from the large-hearted author of "Orion," which he specially prized.

And here I should record that thrilling recital from the platform by W. J. Fox, of "A Coming Cry," with prediction to his hearers that the writer of it might some day rank high, of which I am reminded by Dr. George Bird, a friend and associate of my brother in those days, who, writing to me, vividly recalls his own impressions of his "strange magnetic force, and his eager face lighted up with emotion, and kindling with a '*sæva indignatio*' over the political iniquities of his time."

But his book, which had never been fairly dealt with, fell into utter neglect. With his usual intensity of purpose he had staked all upon this effort, and all had failed.

It was at this time that he looked back upon the path he had trodden for six years, 1837–1843; and the mere disappointment of a literary venture was as nothing to him in comparison with the prescience

of what his life must become should he have, as he
did have, to tread the same path to the end.   Also it
was at this time, or very soon after—that he destroyed
a mass of poetical composition, which he had in pre-
paration for a second volume—had the first succeeded.
This he had intended to style " Studies of Resemblance
and Consent," of which there is some adumbration in
the final poem in his published book.

But having decided to abandon poetry for politics,
he ruthlessly effected this holocaust, lest what he
called his "lust of completion" should tempt him away
from the new path he had chosen, to retouch or complete the many verses he had by him in an unfinished
or imperfect state.

This decision of his was bitterly lamented by me.
I knew that he could force himself, upon a by-path as
it were, into that sphere of activity; since when but a
boy of nineteen he had given proofs of this (one of
which, as I have stated, remains); but he then laid
aside poetical composition only to resume it again.

And I knew still better that the main current of his
thought had been wholly set to poetry, and that only
by following that steadfastly was there any hope of his
distinguishing himself.   This has been proved by the
result.

Work for Cleave and Hetherington, radical publishers
of that day, could only be ephemeral, however ably

performed. His pamphlet on the " Land Monopoly," referred to, and with which he took singular pains, was certain to be void of effect. The political papers he had always on hand, and which he was always modifying and elaborating, never saw the light, and in the end they also were destroyed.

The total divergence of our views at this time had rendered him somewhat rigid on the subject.

For he had forced himself into the belief that it was his duty to place himself on another level of work; and he had the hope, in which I never shared, that he might become instrumental in effecting social good.

Taking therefore, what I thought a favourable opportunity, I ventured to send him the following sonnet—inserted here because it met his eye, and belongs fitliest to this place.

TO THE AUTHOR OF STUDIES OF SENSATION AND EVENT.

No baffling makes the mental conflict vain ;
And province in a realm o'erruling sense
Hath the far-seer ; grandly passing hence,
And dwelling there source-seeking.—We attain
By learning to relinquish—and the strain
Includes the study, when the soul intense
Broodeth o'er shadowy intelligence,
Suddenly procreant—purified through pain.—
And this thou better knowest, and could'st take
Up yet life's heritage of hopes, joys, tears,
And consecrate thee to high tasks, and make
Accomplish'd place, with welcome from thy peers :

Oh ! brother, raise thy voice for Love's dear sake
Who listens, mindful of those early years.

And knowing, as I did, what was in him, I had,
and have, undisturbed, the conviction there expressed.

On another occasion I tried again with the following
verses :

Wings, poet, on thy shoulders bind,
And search the starry heavens to find
   The law that bids thee perish
Unknown, that men of after-days,
When thou art cold to all their praise,
   Thy name may know and cherish ;—

And thou shalt fail :—but acquiesce
Therein, and love thou none the less,
   No thorny crown refusing,
And Fame with ravish'd kiss of fire
Shall consecrate thy love-swept lyre—
   Great thou, without thy choosing.

I am sure that he was not displeased, for he thanked
me, but he remained quietly inflexible, and intimated
that he had other work to do.

Sixteen years afterwards (1860), within a few
weeks of his death, he being then in the bed
from which he was not again to rise, saying sweetly
that he had always liked to hear me read, and talking
politics no more, drew forth a few poems composed in
Jersey during the last winter of his life; and he asked
me to read them out to him. I did so, he observing
that my voice was not so steady as usual, and well it

might fail to be so, while all the past rushed back into
my mind.

It has been incorrectly stated that he "was scarcely
recognisable before he died—a mere ghost and waif
of what he had been but a few years before."* In
the autumn of 1858 he was full of ebullient life, was
hunting anemones with me in St. Brelade's Bay,
Jersey; not that he really cared about them, but at home
we had the sea-water-aquarium-fit on, set going by
Lewes and others; and such was his loving sympathetic
nature† that he said he must contribute a fine "crass"
with his own hands for the "happy family" I was
to take to London; and he did so, sporting in the surf,
with his trousers tucked up, like a happy boy, where
the

> " beach-stones thickly throng'd
> As bright waves o'er them reel."†

And much later on than that he wrote his "Winter
Hymn to the Snow," which has much of his first rapt
love for Nature, and faithfulness to her workings;

---

* Notes and Queries, 4th S. v. 264, March 5, 1870.

† His eldest niece, Eva Mary, who was nearly ten years old
when her gifted uncle died, remembers him very vividly.
She was a great solace to him during the last two years of his
life, and she greatly honours his memory, and speaks of him
as " the most fascinating companion child ever had."

‡ *The Naked Thinker*, p. 4.

and in fact his countenance never showed the ravage of disease that was within, in the chest; and he was abundantly recognisable—as his own old self, I mean, 'sicklied o'er with the pale cast of thought;'—and never more so than when the Angel of Death recognised him, and touched him and took him home.

It must have been in 1856 that he first went to live in Paultons-square. He would pace slowly up and down the sunny side of the square, where any one accustomed frequently to pass at that period must have seen and noticed him; for he was a noticeable man. He had fixed his residence in old Chelsea to be locally associated in that way with Carlyle, whom he looked out for and saw on his rambles in the neighbourhood; but never called upon him, or spoke to him. Reminding him once that in 1843 he sent his "Studies" to Carlyle as an act of homage and reverence, when he hoped to *do* something—I said, "Why not call on Mr. Carlyle? I am sure he would like to see you: you must remember his little note to you in reply, in pure 'Carlylese'—bidding you to 'keep your fire burning, but be careful to consume your own smoke.' He replied,—'I call on Carlyle! see his look fixed on me, and hear his voice uttering the words—'Young man, what have you *done*?' And such a shudder passed over his face, and he was so distressed, that I never renewed the subject. There is something touching in the silent homage he paid to Carlyle.

But Eben had also quite a love for old Chelsea, the old Bridge, and the reaches of the river up to Putney, Kew, Richmond; and after he became too ill to take long walks, he would steal out before bed-time, and loiter on the Bridge and muse; watching the effects of light and shade on those summer nights, when the moon was looking about her, and all was hushed, so that he could hear the water swaying and gurgling among the wooden piles, and mark the craft of the bargemen coming down with the tide. This would often soothe him very much, and then he would go to bed.

I cannot at this moment fill up the interstices of this narrative with further particulars of the later years of my brother's life.

But no sketch, however cursory, should omit to mention by name Mr. W. J. Linton, who was his old associate and friend, and whose heart-felt tribute to his memory finds a place in the present volume. Some of my brother's happiest days were passed as Mr. Linton's guest at Coniston.

A still earlier friend—one who formed part of his life for fully twenty years—"from whom," as Mr. Theodore Watts (whose words I fully endorse) has said, ' he received an infinity of tender kindness,' who stood by him to the last, was his frequent visitor at Paultons-square and at Brentwood (where he was with him till within an hour of his death) and who stood by my side when his body was lowered into the grave—must also be mentioned here.   Any record of my brother would indeed be incomplete that did not contain the name of Horace Harral.

It was early in August 1860, that, yearning for the country once more, he decided to remove to Brentwood, Essex, where a female relative, since deceased, resided, and where he had sisterly attendance too, and every comfort that could be desired for him.   I accompanied him thither.

At first he seemed to rally, his eye still keen and bright, his voice strong ; and he would bid me denote the muscular grasp of his hand, pointing to his chest and saying, " It is only here I fail."   And it was so.

He passed away peacefully on the morning of Friday September 14th, 1860.

He had carefully indicated where he wished to be buried.   " Such reasonably near burying ground as may be at the same time unlikely to be disturbed, and yet not lonesome or neglected," are his words, written by his own hand.   His wish was obeyed.

This true poet sleeps beneath a stone erected to his memory in the rural churchyard of Shenfield, about a mile from Brentwood, in a spot selected absolutely to fulfil his last wish. The stone bears the following inscription :—

SACRED
TO THE MEMORY OF
EBENEZER JONES
SECOND SON OF
ROBERT AND HANNAH JONES
WHO DEPARTED THIS LIFE
SEPTEMBER 14, 1860
AGED 40 YEARS
———
TO LIVE IN HEARTS WE LEAVE BEHIND
IS NOT TO DIE.

The village children pass on their way to school, and the robin perches on the garden fence close beside his grave.

And there may be heard two of his best-loved sounds in life—the watch-dog's bark from the farm across still fields at night, and in Spring-time, in the morning, the throstle's first unmistaking song.

SUMNER JONES.

REMINISCENCES

OF

EBEN JONES.

So many years gone by, no records kept, and dates
not borne in mind, however clear in my own thought
the impression of my friend, I have but an impression,
or some impressions of him, to convey as I best may
to others. Fortunately Mr. Watts's Memoir,* more
authoritative than anything I could give, written
where he has been able to make inquiry of the brother
and other friends, supplies those biographical details
for writing which I should be altogether incompetent.
For I was not even so intimate with Eben Jones as
I have credit for, from his brother Sumner as well as
from others who knew us in our together-time.
Specially referred to as one "who could perhaps give
the best account" of him, his brother kindly endorsing
the words, I am sadly obliged to confess that I can but
poorly meet the claim so made upon me. Would that I
could do more! The theme were worthy of a biographer's

* Printed in *The Athenæum* of Sept. 21, Sept. 28, and
Oct. 12, 1878.—ED.

best powers. There is no change in my affection and esteem for him. After thirty years I may be forgiven some forgetfulness, not effacing nor defacing the impression which remains firmly as fresh stamped upon my soul. Of the man then, rather than of circumstance or event, is what I am able to write.

Companions and close friends for a few years, our lives were sundered, not by any cooling of our friendship. Personal regard most certainly, yet more the similarity of our opinions and our tastes had held us together during our closest years; still it is but simple truth to say, we were hardly so knit together in that closer brotherhood which would deserve the name of intimacy. I say this, not as disclaiming what I had recollected with pride, but as apology for any shortcoming in the words I would write in his praise, for any incompleteness in the portrait I will attempt to draw. Nevertheless I had more than ordinary opportunity of studying, knowing, and esteeming him. How that opportunity taught me I will try to show. If in some respects I may differ from Mr. Watts, or from those who knew him personally better than I, the difference may not invalidate their judgment. Two men looking at a statue from different points may not find it susceptible of precisely the same description; merits or defects may strike either from his standing-place, yet naturally escape the other. Two men seeing the same landscape under perhaps opposite aspects, in light or shadow, in summer or winter, will paint two very dissimilar pictures, though the subject be the same. I apprehend no such great variance between Mr. Watts and myself.

One chief point in so much as it indicates character, to which my attention is first called, is some over-statement, so far as my recollection serves me, as to Jones's despondency and after neglect of poetry on account of the little notice attracted by his first attempt. Particular recollection failing me, I should still know that he was not one to be crushed because, having enlisted among those desirous to make a figure in the world, he found the world in no hurry to witness the performance. Knowing the worth of his attempt, surely he wished for and felt his right to expect some sympathy, if not applause. The desire of appreciation belongs to a healthy mind. But he knew also the course of other poets, and had too much good sense not to be forewarned of his own eventu-alities. His *Studies of Sensation and Event** was published in 1843. John Hamilton Reynolds (Keats's friend and Hood's brother-in-law) in 1814–15, and

---

* I may note in passing that in the copy he gave me he altered the title—then or at a later period—to *Studies of Emotion and Event*. [A similar alteration is made in the title of a copy now in my possession.—ED.]

Charles Wells in 1824, had also published : and were
forgotten, by the critics and by the world.   Hood's
dainty *Midsummer Fairies*, his *Hero and Leander*, his
other serious poems, were forgotten too.   All the
lightness of his so popular humour had been insufficient
to float them into recognition during his life.*
Horne's magnificent tragedies, *The Death of Marlowe*
(1835), *Cosmo de' Medici* (1837), and *Gregory VII.*
(1840), had made no mark above the Lethe flood
of public indifference.   Sarah Flower Adams' *Vivia
Perpetua* (1841) was unknown save to a small circle of
co-religionists.   Ebenezer Elliott was only the poet of
the Corn-Law League, a rhymer in *Tait's Magazine* and
the *Monthly Repository*.   Robert Nicoll died in 1837,
as little cared for outside of Leeds.   Of Wade's *Mundi
et Cordis Carmina* (1835), a book most akin to that of
Jones, I doubt if a score of copies had been sold when
Jones was printing his.   Who were the purchasers of
Darley or of Beddoes ?   I think, recollecting my own
knowledge of those books at that time (I was very
early a hunter of such 'unconsidered trifles') some talk
concerning them must have happened between us, so

---

* I think the first attempt to have him regarded as a poet
rather than as only a humourist was made by my friend
R. H. Horne, in a review of Hood's early volume of poems,
written for the *Illuminated Magazine*, during the few months
in which I succeeded Douglas Jerrold as editor, in 1845.

that they would be known to Jones; and he must have known of them also as not paying speculations and been accordingly prepared for the failure of his own. For that, notwithstanding others' experience, he yet ventured on the same vain quest, who needs to seek a reason? and that not in over-weening conceit of his own ability nor yet in over-sanguineness of nature. The youthful poet must see himself in print. Even the aged may be troubled with the same malady. What crown but one of paper will the voices at the Games award us? After all Chance is mighty. The book *may* sell. At worst there will be presentation copies for appreciative friends: fit audience however few. I call the great God of Poesy and all the Muses to witness that I, who also have published poems, never counted on a sale: not in my youngest days, when I was as aspiring as my friend, more sanguine and more conceited than I knew him to be. My time of companionship with him must have been mainly between 1842 and 1848. I can recal no special alteration of thought or demeanour at all attributable to the non-success of his literary venture. Disappointment struck him in passing, but passed on: having other and more poisoned darts with which to reach him, where no armour of good sense or pride could avail for his protection.

When Hood wrote to Sumner Jones (who, and not

Ebenezer, had forwarded to him a copy of the book)
those harsh words—"shamefully prostituting his gift
of poetical power," because certain of his love-poems,
touched no answering chord in Hood, surely the acknowledgment of poetical power must have satisfied the
poet however the manner of acknowledgment might
hurt the man. It was not in despondency, but with
defiant disdain that Eben met a rebuke so unexpected
and so undeserved. Grieved he doubtless was; grieved
that "impure motive." (other of Hood's words) should
be imputed to him: but it did not make him
"miserable." His answer was a manly letter to Hood,
in courteous, collected, but incisive terms vindicating
himself from a false charge. He was not one to be
cast down by condemnation or to relinquish his right
of self-assertion; nor was he one to be made miserable
by the unjust opinion of any man. Too self-reliant
and with too much pluck for that! Yet in his appreciation of his own genius he wanted not for a manly
modesty, could cordially admire work on a different
plane from his own, and could receive a friendly
criticism as worth attention, for itself or for the critic's
sake. To W. B. Scott, who had promised to send
him a copy of his *Year of the World*, he writes, in a
most characteristic letter :—*

* The substance of this letter was printed in *The Academy*,
November 2, 1878.—ED.

"I think it is about time that I should write to tell you that your proposal to present me with a copy of "The Year of the World"* had been forestalled by Mr. L——'s kindly giving me one. I have delayed doing this because I wanted to write a letter that might accurately represent my regard towards said book and also in some sort reply to your last kind letter to me.

"Touching your remarks on 'Studies of Sensation and Event,' I think they are true; and your qualification of the poems as being true perceptions, "but seen through certain partial conditions of the percipient," very fairly suggests the question whether the condition of the percipient was a condition during which works of art should be undertaken. (Not that I think the poems, except one or two lyrics, worthy of the name of works of art, being so devoid of construction, or constructed with unrecognised material, empty of definite-ness of purpose or unity of representation.) I suppose I need not say that the condition of the percipient generally was 'dissatisfaction,' *backed by determination never to hold one's peace.*

* * * * * * *

"What is literary excellence? Nothing. What is being able to gain the applause of those 'curious in the matters of thought and expression?' Vanity of vanities. What even is influence over the public mind? Why, one must *creep* in order to climb to it, and generally go masked afterwards.

* * * * * * *

"I should be very glad to see you when you come to London.† I suppose you are much older than I am, but I don't think we should be afraid of talking to each other. *I never flourish 'my stake' about.* I see nothing to vaunt in having 'stuck in the mud,' so to speak. *Any sort of beauty, moral or physical,*

---

* *The Year of the World; a Philosophical Poem on "Redemption from the Fall,"* by William B. Scott. Edinburgh and London, 1846, pp. xii. 113. This poem is a descriptive and imaginative expression of the Development theory—not physical but intellectual development : it is based on the perfectibility of human nature.—ED.

† Scott was at this time Master of the School of Design at Newcastle-on-Tyne.

generally puts me in good spirits, so I hope you will not fail
when you come to town to let know

　　　　　　　" Your very honest admirer,
　　　　　　　　　　　" EBENEZER JONES."

The lines I have italicized (the letter was written
in June, 1847) are as windows into the man's heart,
showing us clearly what his nature had : passionate
love of beauty, moral or physical, a self-respect that
forbade him to thrust himself forward for praise or
pity, a stern fortitude that would have refused
commiseration, and a will that knew not how to give
in. There was no sign of yielding even in his saddest
or his weakest days.

Again to make dissentient explanation. I do not
think that Jones's politics were of my manufacturing.
Let him never be confounded with Ernest Jones, *the*
Chartist, and a poet too ; concerning whom, and
marking the difference between the two, I recal some
such words as these :—

　　　　　" Eben Jones,
　　A swift brook among stones ;
　　And less earnest Jones,
　　Scanter brook with more stones."

Eben was a Chartist and he was not a Chartist. A
writer in the *Athenæum* has said :—" Jones, being
a sincere, grave-minded man, not afraid of carrying
out his opinions into their consequences, became a
Chartist."* Let pass the " grave-minded " for the

* *Athenæum*, Sept. 14, 1878.

moment. The "sincere and not afraid" aptly describes the man ; points also to the likelihood of consequence. That "once met by Mr. Rossetti towards 1848," he "would hardly talk on any subject but Chartism,"* means only that he broadly sympathized with the movement; and almost any expression of sympathy was then enough to entitle a man to the name. Mr. Watts is right in saying that "technically" he was not a Chartist: that is to say, I do not think he was ever enrolled as member of any Chartist association or ever (so far as I can call to mind) spoke at a public meeting. Those were days in which that now innocent word Radical meant something exceedingly reprehensible if not actually disreputable : days when to wear a beard or an incipient moustache would call down the condescending scowl of the counting-house Jove, and according to the jovial mood subject you to instant dismissal or the gently severe request that you would leave off that enormity in business hours. So much mercy might be shown if Jove were of the liberal party. Therefore I do not think that Jones would have dared to add to his poetical delinquencies the more noticeable criminality of a speech in public. Dared is however a wrong word here. He dared do anything that he thought right. But he had a certain

---

* *ib., ubi suprà ;* see also Mr. Rossetti's letter in *Notes and Queries*, Feb. 5, 1870.—ED.

practicality and sense of the importance of "minor" duties very remarkable in a poet. Something of the pernicious politics he might have learned from me, in my exceptional position as an artist half-forgiven for "eccentricities" which had damned a young man in the City; but such doctrines were known and felt too generally among the young men of that day, to leave much room for individual credit for conversions. Few of the present generation seem to understand how active the more intelligent of the middle classes were in the agitation, first for the Reform Bill, and afterwards for the Repeal of the Corn Laws; and the sons or younger brothers of those men, yet more enthusiastic or more disinterested than their elders, were Chartists, to the extent Jones was, almost to a man. But the one object on which he cared to concentrate his thoughts (an object too with the Chartists, only too much so, almost to the shelving of the Suffrage question), was the right of the People, instead of a landlord class, to possess the Land. For that he wrote his one sustained prose work. Many short articles also he wrote, most of them in the spirit of *The Kings of Gold*, with burning indignation against the Trader (Reports from Factories and Mines were just then exposing the horrors of those simple organizations of labour), in such wrath as that of Keats, against the men of wealth, in his *Pot of Basil*. Some of these articles, it may be verses also, probably appeared in the *Odd-Fellow* (not named for its comicality, but because it was the record of proceedings of "Odd-Fellows'" Associations), a penny weekly broad-sheet published in the Strand by Henry Hetherington, the gallant and successful champion of the Unstamped Press. Of such appearance there however I cannot speak from certain recollection. I was editor of the *Odd-Fellow* from 1841 to '43, as near as I can recal dates; and when the paper passed out of Hetherington's hands, its named being then changed to the *Fireside Journal* (still with political leaders), Jones became editor in my stead. Whether he wrote only then, or had written before for the *Odd-Fellow* I cannot be sure, not having a single number to refer to; but I suppose his editorship must have been in consequence of assistance given to me in the earlier work. For myself, I wrote political leaders, reviews of books and dramatic criticisms (among them reviews, on first appearance, of Dickens's *Curiosity Shop* and Gerald Griffin's *Gisippus*), poetry, answers to correspondents real or imaginary, anything or everything; and Eben was so much at one with me in all these matters that it seems to me I must have had his occasional collaboration. It is only thus vaguely though that I can speak of his various writing.

His opinions were, as I have said, those of the

Chartist party : going beyond, I would add, to repub-
licanism, but that the prevalent opinions among us all
tended that way if they did not absolutely reach it.
And his opinions were frankly expressed by him when
required.

" Sincere and not afraid :" so, if not of us or among
us, nor technically entitled to the name, he was certainly with us Chartists. The " grave-minded " is not
so applicable a term. Serious, when seriousness was
necessary, would be more exact : for if the other expression implies that he was without a sense of humour
(say rather fun) or a natural tendency to pleasure, it
would altogether mislead. A right capable man of
business, diligent in his hours of work, however *(quasi*
poet) he disliked that work, he could make amends for
the enforced restraint by riotous, almost reckless
enjoyment in the after hours ; could play the bohemian
as well as any never-calvinized youth among us, with
perhaps a more eager craving and fuller relish because
of Calvinistic recollections. That sort of thing may
happen. Grave-minded ? No ! however his spon-
taneity may have been repressed in childish days.
Earnest, intense ! And intense in pleasure also. Every
pore of his being was open to pleasurable sensations,
his attraction generally toward the best. Caught too
readily perhaps (not being suspicious or distrustful)
by a fair outside, loving easily, careless *sometimes* of

appearances (for formality surely he could have no respect), however wilful or careless, I always perceived and respected in him a pure clean-heartedness, a perception of the highest, a severely honest determination to do right, and a chivalrous feeling very rare among men. "He was ever best and happiest," writes his brother Sumner to me, " out of doors ; and the poetic side of his nature then came winningly and delightfully out." Do I not well remember that ? It was no grave-minded man with whom I rambled through our wonderful Lake-Country. His brother, writing but recently, reminds me of a poem called the *Mountain Land*, written after a visit to me at Coniston. My own remembrance dwells most upon our first journey to the Lakes, a week's holiday there from London work. How well to this day I can retrace our steps and recall the pleasant bright companionship that, like the sparkle in the wine, made that pleasure-draught but more enjoyable ; our delight in the moonlight walk from the Windermere Station by the Lake side to Ambleside, that loveliest five miles in all England ; our next day's climb (the track missed) over the Stake Pass, after bathing under the falls in a pool at Great Langdale head ; how we lingered, dallying with our joy, upon the mountain tops till night came on, a cloudy night of late September, after a day of autumn glory, overtaking us before we could reach

the Borrowdale Road ; how, unable even to grope our
way, we lay down together on the stones to sleep, and
awakened by the rain crept under an over-hanging
rock—and, cold and hungry, smoked our pipes and
talked till the dawning light was sufficient for us to
find some trace of path to Stonethwaite ; how we sat
in a cottage porch to await the rising of the inmates
and beg a breakfast of bad coffee and mutton-ham, so
salt that it scarified our mouths.   No grave-minded
man was either of the˙ pair who went laughing and
singing, if somewhat limping on their way ; nor much
was there of a disposition to gravity two evenings later,
when after supper at the little Fish Inn at Buttermere
we amused ourselves with improvising verses (certainly
never printed) not exactly in honour of

> " William Marshall, William Marshall,
>   Cotton-spinner of Leeds ! "

verses of mere rhythmical extravagance, in proper
poetic execration of the factory-owning plutocrat
who had the impudence to possess the one grand home
in beautiful Buttermere.   Full capacity for enjoyment,
whether of his senses or his intellectual faculties,
characterised the man in his day of health : delighted
with all he saw, from the rugged bleakness of Wast-
dale to the pastoral repose of Buttermere, enjoying
equally a row on Crummock-water and our evening
walk beside the golden woods to Keswick.   This was

Ebenezer Jones, the City clerk, not too much disappointed at a literary failure, before his heart was
saddened and his health destroyed.

For it was not that poetic disappointment that
crushed the poetry out of him and broke the brave
man down. Other disappointment, not foreseen or to
be guarded against, heart-sorrow, and disease, pursued
him and marked him for their prey. And then the
home-unhappiness : it is difficult to speak at all of that.
But in barest justice to him something must be said
before I close these insufficient reminiscences. Poetry
he put aside for prose : not altogether. Before all
his ambition was to be a man. To write poetry : yes !
his nature swayed to that, as the tree sways with the
wind, the continual sea-wind that drives all growth in
one direction. The manhood in him refused to be so
bowed and limited. What he might not say, or could
not so well say, in poetry, he would say in prose.
The same knightly desire to battle against Wrong
which produced his *Kings of Gold* impelled his pamphlet
of *The Land Monopoly*. The pleasure-loving poet felt
for the woes of others ; and the ground on which he
wrote is well defined in a single paragraph, when he
writes :—

"In the year A.D. 1846 there were exported from Ireland
3,266,193 quarters of wheat, barley, and oats, besides flour,
beans, peas, and rye,—186,483 cattle, 6,363 calves, 259,257
sheep, 180,827 swine (food that is in the shape of meat and

bread for about one half of the Irish population) ; and yet this very year of A.D. 1846 was preeminently, owing to a Land monopoly, *the famine year* for the Irish people."†

Note the exactness of the man of figures ! Truly a man capable of much beside poetry. As truly at that date, as at some others, something beside poetry was needed. ·Which somewhat concerns poets. This one cared to do his part.

His "day of poetry," the manifestation thereof, was verily, as W. B. Scott has said, "his day of love" : not love of his wife, his volume being published before he knew her, but the earlier love of which Mr. Watts has spoken. Also his genius needed only an occasion (which what impressionable boy has not ?), slight or serious, to provoke its love-dreams. A worshipper of beauty, sensitive, pleasure-loving, impassioned, his erotic poetry was as much the affluence of his blood as of his brain (not that I find one line in it of which one need be ashamed) ; and easily moved to love he could not help but sing, as the buds must open in the spring sunshine. His first title to his book better expressed its genesis than the later title of *Emotion,* perhaps suggested by the unexpected possibility of some mistake as to the meaning of *Sensation.* Also as regards his courtship of the wife, it was too brief for much amount even of the most rapid rhyming. I

† *The Land Monopoly,* p. 10.

believe he had not been many days acquainted with her before, in his impetuous way, taken by some personal attractions and the charm of music, of which he was passionately fond, he proposed and was accepted. Too hasty, alas! Had he rejoiced in a happy home, we had not been without more of such lines as those he did address to her, a richer growth through culture of his most poetic nature, and with the continuance of his day of love continuance of poetic aspiration and a performance only promised by the genuine if not always artistic essays of his youth.

Of the misery of that marriage I must speak. But how? Surely I have no thought of telling the unhappy story after the manner of a witness in a police-court. Trite observations on causes also may be avoided. What would all the facts avail? The facts which I relate bear not the construction which the same facts do reported by any one else. Facts! I never knew any, of man's or woman's life, that could not be stated in at least two ways, and that without direct violation or much straining of the truth. Nay, set down by the Recording Angel himself, were there only the bare record,—we well might dread the Judgment. The outer facts of the life of Sir Philip Sidney, are they not well known to us? And not only the outer facts, but Sidney himself has almost written out the inmost motions of his soul. Some of us can see even in the broadest and plainest statement of the facts nothing but what is in accordance with his loftiest words and confirmation strong as Holy Writ of all we loved to think of England's knightliest son, the idol of his age, " whose life was passed like a summer day, all sunlight, warmth, success, even his death surrounded with the poetic splendours of a summer sunset." Yet by others the same facts have been received as destructive of our ideal, altogether damnatory of the man. I will give no facts. Nor have I word to utter of the wife ; of whom also personally I have but a faint impress, seeing but little of her. I have to write only of what concerns my estimation of the man, of what remains stamped upon my memory as the truth in relation to his conduct and his character. Here is his brother's record. "Ebby, both as boy and man, was full of force and fortitude, and as he advanced in life he became inspired with a high sense of the duty he owed to his fellow men, and was never, *under any trial*—and he had many trials—less than a most genuine, courageous, and uncompromising man, who fought his way back to his Maker, without ever once striking his flag. That was Eben Jones, and in telling you that I tell you what you know." Indeed I know it. And could I ever have had any doubt, that sorest of his trials, how he bore it, and how he behaved, had made me sure. A man most

keenly sensitive, the torture he went through must
have been agony indeed, the bitterest such a man
could undergo.   Like the Spartan lad, he bore the
rending of his bowels without complaint.   I have not
in my mind an instance of heroism more heroic, of
martyrdom more severe than his.   And I speak not
only of the more than Spartan fortitude, but of a
great, unflinching, Christ-like generosity and goodness
which has endeared his memory to me, making of it a
holy thing to which I bow in reverence and love.
What need I of particular facts, happy in forgetting
some ?   The one authentic and well-recognised like-
ness of my friend lives before me ; and no portrait,
nor other identified facts, can make me think it false.

Looking back among other memoranda I find that
I must have begun my acquaintance with Eben in
1842.   In the beginning of that year I became the
partner of John Orrin Smith, the engraver, of whom
Horace Harral had been a pupil.   Working daily
beside each other, both young men, Harral and I were
friendly ; and he soon introduced me to Jones.   So
also I knew Sumner Jones, and can recollect how we
four spent many an evening together.   Of the merit
of Sumner Jones, a poet also, but of a more retired
and contemplative disposition, as he is still living, it
would be impertinent here to speak ; and it was
Eben toward whom my sympathies were chiefly

drawn, and whom in consequence I better knew. How we drifted apart I hardly recall to mind. It was not purposely. In 1844 I was busied with Mazzini in bringing before Parliament our complaint of the opening of letters in the English Post-Office. That led to friendship with the great Italian, and involved me later in European politics, making large demands upon my time ; also heavily taxed (Mr. Smith dying in 1845) by the sole charge of a business on which two families depended. I can find no other reasons except this want of time to account for any discontinuance of the always friendly and at one time very frequent intercourse between myself and Jones. In 1849 I removed to the North, and after that engrossing political work, then sorrows of my own, had share in sundering us. For years I had seen and heard but little of him till returning to London, I learned that he was living in Paultons-square, Chelsea, and went to see him. I found him dying : the wreck of his old energetic self, wasted away, sad, but uncomplaining. That evening no one was with him but his son, a delicate nervous boy, little able to be of comfort to the life-wearied man. I believe that even then Jones was engaged on some accountant's work, with his old pride, to eat only the bread of independence. He gave me, almost as a parting gift, some three or four short poems, written no great while before.

They are somewhere, among other treasured papers, letters and other relics, which one religiously preserves yet dares not look at. I have them not in this country, and know not how to direct anyone to find them. I speak of them but to prove that through all unhappiness, even to the last, the poetic spirit had not departed from him. Even to the last. A few days later he had left London, to lay his bones at Shenfield.

Sensations of the keenest, whence quick impulses; clear insight as to right and wrong, from which arose his indignation against injustice; fearlessness and fortitude, and with them tenderness for others; rare poetic gifts, and at the same time the practical talent and good sense of a man of the world : all these belonged to Ebenezer Jones. What he has written speaks for itself, needs no comment, eulogium or criticism from me. I have spoken only of the man. He was of the type of Alcibiades, but with an idea of duty which the Greek had not: a man seemingly marked out from his birth, by his very nature, to be beloved and to succeed. Sorrow and Misfortune saw and envying slew him. Only a memory remains in place of all that promise.

W. J. LINTON.

NEW HAVEN, CONN., U.S.A.
March, 1879.

[NOTE.—Most faithful are the "Reminiscences" of my brother which Mr. Linton has sent across the Atlantic, but as might be expected from that blissful unconsciousness of the realities of City life in which artists and men of letters can rejoice, a few qualifying words are here and there required. I confirm Mr. Linton's conjecture that my brother never made "a speech in public." Had he done so, however, it would not have been "to add to poetical delinquencies" in the City ; for, with that "practicality and sense" to which Mr. Linton refers as "very remarkable in a poet," he preserved the line of demarcation between City work and poetical or political activity so complete, that to this day I meet occasionally those who knew him in the haunts of business, and remember him well as an able man of affairs, yet who are quite unconscious that anything better than invoices or commercial correspondence ever passed his pen. The moral obliquity of City life, his groove of it and mine, with him and since, can only be described by those behind the scenes—record of which exists, but of that this is not the place to speak. He knew that to be in the City is not to be of it. To serve is not to share, and the soul need contract no stain. Many a City clerk can say "Amen" to that, though it may be long before one like my brother shall step from his desk to Paternoster-row, and publish over his own name his defiance to the Mammon-worshippers, returning thence only to see that "shattering of his ideal" of a nobler brotherhood elsewhere, on which Mr. Watts has written with such absolute grasp of truth.

It may here give a tinge of biographical interest to state that my brother made more than one effort at escape. In 1846 (the Railway-mania year) he became for a time the secretary of a Railway Company, which soon collapsed. Again, when the *Daily News* was established, he endeavoured to join the staff of that newspaper, and I saw an interchange of letters between my brother and Mr. Dickens on the subject ; but he was referred from one to another, and in the end nothing came of that.

Yet he would, in one way or another, inevitably have freed himself, had it not been for incessant and extravagant claims upon him, thwarting at every turn one who to work with high-minded men would have been content to live upon the ascetic edge of life. On that subject—the deep domestic calamity—I restricted myself to the one word "lamentable," lest kindred feeling might be supposed to guide a partial pen, and also because I dared not trust myself to speak.

Mr. Linton, without hint from me, has spoken out. I know all that he has set down, and more—know the duty done to the uttermost, the suffering silently borne, the sacrifice of himself in ceaseless striving to reclaim.

For him there is no more grief.

But I cannot rest without telling Mr. Linton in this note how great the solace is to me, and will be until my time comes to pass away, to find that such sorrow was confided to such sympathy, to one who knew so well how to "guess at the wound and heal with secret hand."

We have all our differing estimates of things—in poetry as in politics. With my brother, his politics sprang out of his poetry, and poetry in itself was little or nothing to him otherwise than as a form of *life*, the secret issues of which are in the heart of man.

There was no "lost leader" for my brother in Mr. Linton. I knew from a letter he sent to him, not long before he went to Brentwood to die, how he held him in his inmost heart. Nearly nineteen years have passed away, and now I know the response he met, and it is sacredly dear to me.

And surely all can agree that such things as these, between such men as my brother was and as Mr. Linton is (let the reader turn to his words), may be, in a reckoning not ours, better than song, and ten times more than fame.—S. J.]

Studies of Sensation and Event.

[Published 1843.]

[*Studies of Sensation and Event ; Poems, by Ebenezer Jones. London: Charles Fox, Paternoster Row.* MDCCCXLIII. The text of the present reprint is founded on two copies of the original Edition, marked throughout with autograph corrections by the author. The dedication to Shelley is now printed for the first time from one of these copies.]

TO THE MEMORY OF

SHELLEY

WHO DIED 8TH JULY 1822

BUT WHO LIVETH FOR EVER

IN THE HEARTS AND MINDS OF POETS

I INSCRIBE THIS BOOK

NOT SO MUCH IN REVERENCE

FOR HIS PERFECTION IN ART

AS IN LOVE OF THE INFINITE GOODNESS

OF HIS NATURE

IN WHICH PARTLY FOR ITS ESSENTIAL BEAUTY

AND PARTLY BECAUSE IT WAS HUMAN

IT HAS OFTEN BEEN GIVEN ME TO REJOICE

WITH JOY UNSPEAKABLE AND FULL OF GLORY

"The great end of all the arts is to make an impression on the imagination and the feeling. The imitation of nature frequently does this. Sometimes it fails, and something else succeeds. I think, therefore, the true test of all the arts is, not solely whether the production is a true copy of nature, but whether it answers the end of art, which is to produce a pleasing effect upon the mind."

SIR JOSHUA REYNOLDS.

THE NAKED THINKER.

THE house was broad, and squared, and high,—
   The house of Apswern's lord,—
And all the lordly houses nigh
   Did with its forms accord ;
Their portals all four steps did dwell
   Above the drifting crowd,
And all their windows did repel,
   Deep set, and heavily brow'd ;
The house was one of countless ones,
   All builded white with stone ;
And round its base for ever runs
   The hurrying people's tone.

The room was wholly bare, and raised
   Above all other rooms,
And its large crystal window gazed
   O'er roofs, and towers, and domes ;
The winds uncheck'd around it swept ;
   And o'er all others high,
Straight into it the sunshine stept
   Stark naked from the sky ;
'Twixt it and the revolving stars
   Did never aught arise,
And morning's earliest golden bars
   Its walls did first surprise.

Now forward in this lonely room,
   A door unsounding swings—
White human movings just illume
   The darkness whence it springs ;
The darkness dies, without the door,
   A man half naked stands ;
His eyes are fix'd with thoughtful lore,
   Baring himself, his hands :
And down into this lonely room,
   As swimmer unto sea,
With stately tread, defying head,
   All naked steppeth he.

Twelve times this lonely chamber round
    This naked man doth pace,
His globing eyes growing more profound,
    Scorn firing more his face ;
Each grand limb firmly planting franks
    Itself its place's lord ;
His body, from its haughty flanks,
    Lifts like a lifted sword ;
He pauses, and like one who stands
    Trampling an emperor's crown,
He lifteth high his clenched hands,
    He strains his stern limbs down.

Before the room's large window'd eye,
    That stares from roof to floor,
He stands ; the sunshine from the sky
    Dazzlingly slants him o'er :
With splendid perfectness the sheen
    Kills every shade and haze,
And multitudinous and keen
    His bossed form displays :
Loud laughs he at the sounding crowd
    That far beneath him tides,
Chariots, and dames, and horsemen proud,
    Corpses, and harlots, and brides.

An infant's laugh's a blessed thing,
　　Its soft fall smooths the soul;
And children's laughter, when they spring
　　Away from loved control;
Such laughs are but the gentle lift
　　Of gently joy-breezed life:
This man's bare laughter, hard and swift,
　　With scorn's delight was rife;
His muscles glisteningly unthong'd
　　As burst each ringing peal,
And shone like beach-stones thickly throng'd
　　When bright waves o'er them reel.

While sinks this scornful laughter down
　　Deep in his frame, to thought,
He turns from gazing o'er the town
　　Like one by ghosts besought;
He couches on the chamber's floor,
　　His limbs like creatures spread;
And writes he jest, or writes he lore,
　　He writes with thought-stoop'd head;
And ever and anon, while glides
　　Over the scrolls his pen,
He stops, and glisteringly rides
　　His laughter forth again.

Why seeks this man this lonely height
　　His fellows sport below !
Why is he naked, what doth he write,
　　Nakedly couching low ?
What mean the scorns that swiftly surge
　　O'er his expanded eyes ?
Why do his mind-strung muscles urge ?
　　What is their mind's emprize ?
What means the room, of life's stuff bare
　　As mountain-hollow'd grave ?
The naked manhood, nerving there,
　　Like a tongue in its dark red cave ?

The abbey-bell toll'd fast and loud
　　When Apswern's old lord died ;
And all the people rose and bow'd,
　　And mourn'd their nation's pride ;
He had led its armies through the world,
　　Like sea-snakes through the sea ;
And he its flags of peace unfurl'd
　　While earth blazed up her glee ;
The bell of the abbey heavily toll'd,
　　When they bore his corpse to its tomb ;
And the thought of death did arise and fold
　　The thought of God with its gloom.

But when Apswern's old lord died,—
   When pale on his couch he lay,
So that the gazer might not decide
   What of him was life, and what clay,—
When the weeping servants distant stood,
   And the tearless loving stood near,—
When the doctor's eye forgot to brood,
   Regaining human fear,—
When the frighten'd people in whispers spake
   Of the fears that they could not disclose,
As children do who in darkness wake—
   The Lord of Apswern arose :

And he said, " They think me great and proud,
   Their kings have knelt to me ;
Before me ranks of manhood bow'd,
   Their looks no more were free :—
I die a fool, a duping fool ;
   I leave a veiled world,
Wherein, by unsuspected rule,
   I thought no veils were furl'd ;
I sink within the senseless tomb,—
   The shapes I seem to leave
Now shake their masks, and midst the gloom
   Some real glimpses give.

" Duped, unsuspecting, from my birth
    Till now, my life has been ;
And yet I flaunted o'er the earth,
    As I all truths had seen ;
I thought I fought for man,—I know
    'Twas for the thing man seem'd ;
I thought to man my love did flow,—
    It flow'd to dreams I dream'd ;
With armies I have lash'd the world,
    And at my will it flew,
I knew not what the power I hurl'd,
    Nor that I did subdue.

" I die deceived ;—but one shall tear
    The masks that lied to me ;
The lands that I bequeath mine heir,
    He but retains, while he
Fights with his eyes against the world,
    Against all things that are,
Mocking the veils around them furl'd,
    And scattering them afar ;
Through him I hurl detecting scorn
    At life's old harlot zone,
I crush her masks for centuries worn,
    I strip her on her throne.

" Let there be lifted from the roof
   Of Apswern's house, a room
From every other room aloof,
   And bare as is the tomb;
And stripp'd of all the clothes we wear
   To aid life's lying show,
Naked from every influence, there
   Lord Apswern's heir must go;
And there, alone, for Apswern's land,
   A tenth of each day war
Fiercely to rend life's seemings and
   Drag out the things that are."

Long ere the worms had fretted through
   The clay that thuswise spake,
The heir's dependents swiftly flew
   His lonely room to make;
With wanton jests, with reasons wise,
   They forced him there each day;
That he might seem in legal eyes
   His fortune's price to pay:
Lord Apswern holds that old man's land,
   He works that old man's will;
But now, though bound him no command,
   He'd work that wild will still.

For minds that underneath the blaze
   Of Time's revolving things,
Have learn'd to spurn what world-shared rays
   The troop, quick passing, flings—
And stopping each, with stern command,
   Have forced it to disclose
Its inmost soul, the unknown land
   It comes from, where it goes,—
Can no more calmly passive lay
   'Neath what things seem, than can
Eagles, who've track'd the sun's bright way,
   Stare at it, down with man.

And thus, though bright through Kensington
   Lord Apswern's fellows stray,
Ladies with beauteous garments on,
   And lords, with laughter gay ;
Making not sense a sword to tease,
   Or fight the summer day,—
The day, a sunny bright sea-breeze,
   That breeze's bright spray, they ;
Though thus through Kensington they glide,
   While bright their light smiles play,
No thoughts to strive with, or deride,
   And happiness all their way ;—

This day that joys Lord Apswern's peers,
    And seeks his lonely room,—
He heeds not, though alone it rears
    Its face there, bright with bloom;
Working his work, with painful throes,
    He broods, and writes, and raves,—
Kensington's music towards him flows,
    He smiles not o'er its waves;
His body writhes beneath his strife
    To make men keenlier see;—
Not for the glory of all his life
    Should any I love be he.

Lord Apswern's eyes are lightning keen,
    So keen his world is not
The world by other mortals seen,
    His thought is not their thought:
Lord Apswern glows with glorious pride,
    That lift beyond earth's creeds,
Its thoughts and laws beneath him tide,
    Hour storms he calmly reads;—
But ever in courts, in marts, in farms,
    Whether we joy or moan,
Yea, even in the lovingest lady's arms,
    Lord Apswern is alone.

THE WAITS.

I HAD seen the snow sink silently to the ground;
　　And beauteously its white rest
Quieted all things; and the hushing sound
Murmuring and sinking everywhere around,
　　Blessed me and was blest.

I had seen the moon peep through the dark cloud-flight,
　　Then gradually retreat;
And her re-appearing smile of gentlest might,
Beneath which all the clouds sank calm and bright,
　　Me lustrously did greet.　　　.

And I had heard the ungovernable sea
　　Earth's quietness loud scorn;
I had mark'd afar his raging radiancy,
And proudly, in his pride, had felt that he
　　And I were twain god-born.

But than the under-uttering hush of snow,
   Than the moon's queenly reign,
Than ocean's pride, more beautiful did glow
One other beauty,—even now bending low
   I adore to it again.

For on that night, while Christmas melody plain'd
   Our lonely house around,
Interpreting wild feeling, else restrain'd
From any utterance in the heart death pain'd ;—
   Suddenly, hushing sound,

Came from a lonely chamber's opening door
   A beautiful boy child ;
His pale face fear'd to dare the darkness more,
His white feet hesitated o'er the floor,
   And many a prayer he smiled.

Then tiptoe gliding through the gallery's gloom,
   His hands press'd on his heart,
Noiselessly enter'd he a distant room,
And stealthily its mellow'd moonlight bloom
   His gliding limbs did part ;—

Till o'er a couch all bathed in slanting sheen,
    Where, lapt in splendour, slept
A little girl her childhood's sleep serene,—
His look growing like to her look, he did lean,
    And a brief moment kept

Affection fixed, a reposing gaze
    Upon the sleeping light,
Pleasuring beneath her eyes, and like soft haze,
O'er the clueless beauty of her mouth's sweet maze,
    Glowing mildly bright.

When suddenly, with intenser utterance, scream'd
    The music's wild require ;
And as suddenly his startled countenance beam'd
In vivid pallor, and his wide eyes gleam'd
    With coming and going fire :—

And then he arrested her unclasped hand,
    He kiss'd her gentle cheek ;
Till sighing, as loth to leave sleep's peaceful land,
Her eyes look'd sadly up, and wearily scann'd
    His face, while he did speak.

                                        C

He whisper'd, "Hark ! the music that you fear'd
   Again we might not hear ;
Wake ! wake ! it is very passionate, it has near'd—
It mourneth, like the wind o'er the moors career'd—
   Listen ! listen ! Amabel dear."

Here ! here ! that beauty, which than hush of snow,
   Than the moon's royal reign,
Than ocean's pride, more beautiful did glow,
He is that beauty ; even now bending low,
   I adore to it again.

Sweet peace to me the hushing snow had sent,
   The moon had given me joy,
The ocean transport ; but high thought-content,
Begotten of all things, measureless, yet unspent,
   Gave me this gentle boy.

For, from the sanctuary of this scene,
   Through the strange world around,
That never knew happiness, that fierce and mean,
Now whiningly grovelleth, with disease unclean,
   That deepening, owns no bound ;—

Where love loud rages, seeing throned the wrong
   That all his hope destroys ;
Where poetry pales, despairing, and for song
Raves, till her utterance, erst so sweet and strong,
   Sinks to mere maniac noise ;

Where even science hath fall'n, with terrible dread
   Palsied his strenuous limbs,
Dashing the diadem from his anguish'd head,
And howling atheist howlings—was I led ;
   And, lifting solemn hymns,

Nor anger moved me, nor disgust, nor scorn,
   Nor suffer'd I any fear :
For when the drear was stormiest, most forlorn,
This boy illumined, soft his voice was borne,
   "Listen, listen, Amabel dear."

A DEATH-SOUND.

OH ! never sent Italian summer a fairer, brighter day,
Than when amid the wildwood he led young Rose
away ;
Down from heaven's curving roof of all unshaded blue
Sank the sunshine o'er the hills, and strong the forest
through ;—
All the leaves did droop, and all the birds did dream;
They pass'd the silvery fishes, slumbering on the
stream ;
'Twas the fearfully bright noon-hour, and restless life
had gain'd
Its most unshelter'd pinnacle, and failed rapture pain'd ;
    For the press of the sunshine held the world ;
    And with never a breeze or a sound,
    The golden air glow'd radiant,
    While as ever the earth rush'd round.

Down- all the happy morning the birds did flit and
    sing ;
But now across the silence there waved not any wing ;
They were sitting 'neath the trees, he felt her soft
    hand come,—
It clasp'd his brow and swerved it towards her bosom
    home ;
He sank upon his pillow, resign'd to think that this,
If bliss might be on earth, was sure earth's happiest
    bliss :
Then heard he through her frame the busy life-works
    ply,
But the sound was not of life ; and he knew that she
    must die :
    And the press of the sunshine held the world ;
    And with never a breeze or a sound,
    The golden air glow'd radiant,
    While as ever the earth rush'd round.

" Why start you so?" she whisper'd ; no words found
    he to say ;
" You are pale, you are chilly, love ?"—again her lips
    did pray ;
He urged his ear into her bosom,—fast the life-works
    ply,

But the sound was not of life,—he was sure that she
   must die ;
The life within his veins did press at every pore,
He found no speech, and warm he felt her tear his
   cheek drop o'er,—
One tear, and then another ;—Oh, it seem'd death
   dared not be,
And he laugh'd, "I am well, I am well, I ever grow
   with thee :"
     And the press of the sunshine held the world ;
     And with never a breeze or a sound,
     The golden air glow'd radiant,
     While as ever the earth rush'd round.

Now distant wedding-bells rang out ; he saw her
   blushing cheek,—
Of their coming bridal morning she thought that he
   might speak :—
'Twas then his brain sank broken ; Oh, seek no more
   to know ;—
The worms will make their feast upon her coffin'd
   brow ;—
When she died in his arms, "forget, forget," she said,
"How I loved thee, love thee dying," then her last
   look fed,

And died against his face ; Oh ! is there reason why
Haunts me that summer morning, when he found
   that she would die ;
     When the press of the sunshine held the world ;
     And with never a breeze or a sound,
     The golden air glow'd radiant,
     While as ever the earth rush'd round.

ZINGALEE.

THE war was over ; the ship
Sail'd gaily towards the land ;
He leap'd upon the deck,
Joy-fire in his face and neck ;
A tear his cheek did fleck
As he murmur'd softly "land,"
" Her land !" " her land !"
His colour burned high,
His look assured the sky,
Then glanced exulting scorn,
When, on that joyous morn,
Away, away, through the dazzling spray,
He sprang from the ship to the roaring sea,
And seized the waves in their savage play,
And rush'd with their rush, more bright than they ;

Zingalee !

A myriad eager men,
Thronging the harbour mound,
With flags of fights sublime,
With a myriad church-bell chime,
Hail his returning time,
And loud his victory sound :
    Bare-limbed stand,
    In dazzling band,
    The noblest ladies of the land,
      Gracing his car ;—
Their white breasts bend, their arms ascend,
And their eyes extend, towards his ship afar ;
And their gentlest musics and softest voicings
O'erpower the sense with intense rejoicings ;
But away, away from this proud array,
In lonely delight to his bride bounds he ;
No lady-abandonment wins him to stay ;
He reck'd nought of power, or of glory that day ;
                Zingalee !

He has leaped from the brine ;
His visage smiles divine ;
The flashings of its light
Change, change, more bright, more bright,
As dawn upon his sight,

Remember'd things that sign
Her shrine !
'Twas here farewells were dreaded,
'Twas here farewells were spoken,
And here farewells were hushed,—
Here anew wild they wedded,
Here gave they the love-token,
And here the last grief gushed,
  At their parting time !
  And now to acclime
His gasping life to the heaven it nears,
Here he takes the love-token she gave with tears,—
Her pictured self, as o'er him she hung,
When her love from her loveliness all veil flung,
" Drawn by herself," so its jewels tell,
" For one whom none other can love so well :"
And calm'd is his face, bliss-ful are his eyes,
While over the picture low murmureth he,
With voice whose deep love signeth sweet self-sur-
 prise,
" Was I ever away from this paradise ?"
        Zingalee !

And bright with the glowing repose
Of one long dwell'd in heaven,

To whom assurance great
Of the unchanging fate
Binding his blissful state,
Suddenly has been given,—
He passeth the garden where nestles her home ;
And fondly he noteth the roses, like foam
Flecking the greenery round ;
The birds softly warbling, the breeze waving treen,
The atmosphere sunny, the heaven serene,
And the sea's distant sound ;
Oh ! he noteth them all as parts of her,
With her, through them, doth his soul confer,
    For she loves them all ;
He enters the mansion, with quivering frame
He glides to her chamber, soft murmuring the name
    She was used him to call :
  There heard he a sound
  That lovingly wound
  Wild words around ;—
  'Twas her voice—
  And faintly it said,
  " Oh ! nothing I dread,
  But that thou mayest be fled ;
  No ! bid me rejoice ;
Let me fly with thee even to the end of the world,
But my life must, must ever in thy life be furl'd,

I cannot even die, from thee parted :"
And he stagger'd towards the room,
And there, in voluptuous gloom,
Her breasts all naked and heaving,
    Lay his bride ;
    And her beside
One like a man, around him cleaving
Her quivering limbs, while still she moan'd grieving,
"I cannot even die from thee parted."
    The river of his life stood still,
      Rose at its woe,
    And gazed with terrible will
      The abysm below :—
A wild beast he rush'd to the couch where now grows
The deep stillness of love-rite; back, hissing, shrank he;
One long deepening howl from his crashing life rose ;
Convulsed, he fell senseless ; his wrenched face froze,
Where still linger'd the sound of her wanton love-
    throes :—

              Zingalee !

He is born ; again he is born ;
And unto his life of woe
He awakeneth slow,
Moaning low :—

He hath no soul for scorn ;
His mind nought questioneth, he is alone,
Staring past everything, unmoved as stone,
 As cold.—
Over his hand hath fallen her love-token ;—
He seeth it, his despairing trance is broken,—
He calleth on his love, his love, his love ;
Down on his knees, with clasped hands he calleth,
Upon his love, upon his love, upon his love ;—
But no quick footstep to his couch'd ear falleth,
Only the voice-disturbed tapestries move :
 He bounds to the air ;
 Oh ! music is there,
And he gnashes his teeth, and teareth bare
His bosom, and grovelleth on the ground
His naked flesh, and howleth around :—
He flies to the jessamine bower, where first
On one golden eve his passion outburst ;
Fair, fair to his thought that heaven-time glows,—
There oft in her arms did his life repose,
'Twas there, in the flush of their youthful pride,
He walk'd a god, and she, his bride,
Some robeless nymph, sported with flowers,
Dancing her joy through summer hours.
Still in thought he beholds her thus playfully pace,
But another burns at each naked grace ;

And another seeks, with the flowers she wove,
To fetter her flight, and constrain her to love :—
The flesh flakes on his face !
His eyes roll blood-blind !
A corpse stands in his place !
Its joints knock in the wind !
And across the joyous town,
Over the pastures brown,
Beneath the sunny skies,
The gibbering thing doth flee :—
Dead on the moor it lies,
Cover'd with worms and flies ;

　　　　　　　　　　　　　　Zingalee !

Why weeps Zingalee ?
　　Words only conceal,
　　Thought cannot reveal
　　The tortures they feel
Who suffer as suffered he :—
But even didst thou know
The worst of his woe,
Still shouldst thou not, Zingalee, weep ;
For thy tears might cheat his soul from its͏̄rest
To love thee still, and be still opprest,
　　　Seeing thee love another ;—

Oh ! thou must not weep, thou must seem to scorn
His love and his woe, and from morn to morn
    All grief must thou smother :—
Then crown thee, then crown thee with jewels bright,
And with joyous robes thy body bedight,
Summon thy music, illumine thy hall,
Dance and exult, like a young bacchanal,
Greet thy live lover with love's wild glee,
                    Zingalee !

EMILY.

Oh listen, nymphs! to my distress;
Tell Emily! tell what wild desire
Throbs all my veins, and yet confess
I would not lose the glorious fire.
Oh listen, nymphs! in sunny wind,
Emily on the lawn reclined;
One of her beauteous arms was wound
Embracingly her pillow round;
Her face and bosom, 'neath the sky,
Backwardly loll'd, in smiles did lie;
Her face and bosom upward bending
Flush'd as with virgin shames; and lending
Her hand to some caressing dream,
Over her flowing limbs it lay,
Where stricken by the sunny beam,
Around it rosy light did play:
And seem'd those gently swelling limbs,

Curving at sound of warm love-hymns,
Towards fond minglement, though they
Minglement made not, but did stray
Partedly ever ; and the dress
Which fell soft o'er this loveliness,
Its glowing life all unconcealing,
Yet shaded from entire revealing,—
With witching modesty confessing
What matchless splendour still it veil'd,
Though oft the breezes, rudely pressing,
The heavenly secrecy assail'd,—
And then illumed the couch of azure,
And then the air did pant and glow,
While shivering with mysterious pleasure,
Like waves her limbs did lift and flow.

Oh listen, nymphs ! the sound of horn,
Over the distant mountains borne,
Disturb'd her dream ; Oh marvellous grace !
She moved, she raised her brightening face ;
She rose against the lipping wind,
So fondly its persistings wrestling,
I almost thought she still design'd
Still to endure its boisterous nestling.
Glowing she sate ; her lustrous eyes

D

Gave trusting thoughts to far-off skies,
And sometimes glancing o'er our earth,
Bless'd it with smiles whole empires worth,—
Such proud, bright, wild, caressing smiles,
With pride and love so sweetly blended,
That ever, when her gaze ascended,
I watch'd for one of Nature's wiles
To lure it back ;—or blackbird's singing,
Or childhood's shout through far woods ringing.

I glided towards her, hush'd were words,
By her I knelt ;—to list the birds
To watch the sky like her I strove,
But could not, all my life did love :—
I could but gaze her blissful cheek,
The heaven of her brow I could but seek,—
The slightest varying of her look,
The gentlest movement of her form,
My nature to its centre shook
With rapturous agony ; a storm
Of joy rush'd o'er my startled being.--
Giving me all her gaze, and seeing
My quivering face, her eyelids fell,
Swift to her brow the crimson flew,
Her bosom heaved, her throat did swell,

Around her mouth a new smile grew;
Gasping, I sank upon the ground,
Powerless of sign, or sight, or sound.

Upon that ground her robe was spread,
And on that robe was lain my head;
Into its folds, burningly yearning,
My lips went, pouring kisses, till
I shook with ecstasy, and felt
The pulses of my life sink still,
And every energy to melt.
Time was not then; how long I lay
'In that sweet death, not mine to say; ·
From 'neath my cheek did something move;—
Arising was my worshipp'd love;—
Swift to my mind a strange thought darted,
And wildly to my feet I started,
"Where lay my cheek?"—I trembling said;—
Back three steps stepp'd the blushing maid,—
A short soft laugh betray'd her joy,
Her fingers with their rings did toy,
With smiling eyes the ground she eyed,
And "on my foot" her voice replied.
Then forward that divinest foot
With the same short soft laugh she put;

I saw the sandals gaily lacing
Its gracefully arched instep ; yearn'd—
Whilst sportively the flowers displacing,
It stroked slow the turf, whilst turn'd
Its smooth round ankle, very slowly,
Its inside curve out, askingly—
That it and I again were lowly,
My cheek upon it taskingly ;
My lips again its smoothness pressing,
While conscious what they were caressing.
Oh ! doubt not how I strove to gain
Emily's grace ; all, all was vain ;
Laughter alone was her reply ;
"I die," I moan'd,—she whisper'd, "die ;"
Still smiling smiles, she backward drew,
And bade me stay, and homeward flew.
Upon the couch where she had lain
I sprang ; it but increased my pain ;
And where her cheek had press'd the pillow
I buried mine ; a little billow
Of dew-gemm'd velvet told me where
Her breath had fall'n, and of her hair
I found the odour ;—far I flew,
Still she pursues, and still I her pursue.
Oh ! when was wretchedness like mine ?
Never may I be self-forgiven ;

Encouch'd upon that foot divine,
Yet ignorant that I was in heaven !
Tell, tell me, nymphs ! what hopes have I ?
For this, for this, did Emily fly.

THE HAND.

Lone o'er the moors I stray'd;
With basely timid mind,
Because by some betray'd,
Denouncing human-kind;
I heard the lonely wind,
And wickedly did mourn
I could not share its loneliness,
And all things human scorn.

And bitter were the tears
I cursed as they fell;
And bitterer the sneers
I strove not to repel;
With blindly mutter'd yell,
I cried unto mine heart,—
" Thou shalt beat the world in falsehood,
And stab it ere we part."

My hand I backward drave
As one who seeks a knife ;
When startlingly did crave
To quell that hand's wild strife
Some other hand ; all rife
With kindness, clasp'd it hard
On mine, quick frequent claspings
That would not be debarr'd.

I dared not turn my gaze
To the creature of the hand ;
And no sound did it raise,
Its nature to disband
Of mystery ; vast, and grand,
The moors around me spread,
And I thought, some angel message
Perchance their God may have sped.

But it press'd another press,
So full of earnest prayer,
While o'er it fell a tress
Of cool soft human hair,
I fear'd not ;—I did dare
Turn round, 'twas Hannah there !

Oh ! to no one out of heaven
Could I what pass'd declare.

We wander'd o'er the moor
Through all that blessed day ;
And we drank its waters pure,
And felt the world away ;
In many a dell we lay,
And we twined flower-crowns bright ;
And I fed her with moor-berries,
And bless'd her glad eye-light.

And still that earnest pray-er
That saved me many stings,
Was oft a silent sayer
Of countless loving things ;—
I'll ring it all with rings,
Each ring a jewell'd band ;
For heaven shouldn't purchase
That little sister hand.

TWO SUFFERERS.

'NEATH an Acacia's overhanging branches,
That venture not to touch it; where the ground
Is carpeted richly with the sumptuous greenness
Of soft moss clustering ;—tall, in graceful youth,
With gentleness about its countenance,
And mild reserve, as though itself it lifted
To find retirement from intrusive herbs
Around it sprawling in indelicate joy,—
The alone star of a large ancient garden,
A spotlessly white lily gleam'd : at morn,
Leading the orisons of all the flowers,
Soft its voice rose ; when the hot noonday sun
Was troubling every leaf to pleasant pain,
Often o'erwearied spirits of the breeze
Lapsed towards its sphere, and, softly bending forward,
It seem'd to tremble joyfully, the while
They sank beside its fragrance ; and at even,
When the gently pressing dusk awoke to revel,
Those not-perceived beautiful ones, who frolic

In old umbrageous woods, whence swift they rush
Out on fields moonlight-bathed, to startle back
In pleasing fear, who know the thoughts of flowers,
Loving them more than man does,—there did visit it
Troops of these gentle creatures, and they stay
Each other to admire it, some entreat
The wind to wave back the acacia boughs
That screen it from the moonlight, others around it
Press the elastic turf in lightsome dance,
Or rest reclining, whilst all night it smiled
The same mild smile : but neither morning's flowers,
Who ceased their hymns to listen to its music
So soft and full ; nor spirits of the breeze,
Who, fainting in its shadow, gain'd fresh strength
Contemplating its grace ; nor woodland nymphs,
Who for its gentle smile selected it
The witness of their loves and revelry ;
Dream'd—that within the centre of its roots
Ravaged a fierce and unopposed destroyer,
Gnawing with venomous teeth its shuddering core,
Sleeplessly raging.

Distant a moth-flight from this suffering lily,
Centred amidst vast interbranching treen,

A temple of pleasure glowed with the light
Dazzlingly undulating it within
Ever with varying hue,—now azure, now roseate,
Now yellow as amber ; like one gorgeous opal
It glow'd, and in its vast capaciousness
Exquisitely nerved life sought all sensations,
Crises, and tides of pleasures.   Festival
Had summon'd there beauty and youthfulness,
The gentle and the gallant ; its broad mirrors
The company multiplies, the space disbounds,
And its music strangely wantoneth, and aye changeth
The hue of its light,—till pleasingly bewilder'd
Its revellers doubt the earthliness of the scene,
All precedent circumstance dazzled from their thought,
All future.   Suddenly the music sinks ;
Each knight prays to some lady, and with smiles
And downcast eyelashes, and fluttering body,
Each lady grants the prayer ; and gently laughing
Low, tumbling laughter, gives her beautiful self
To his disposal, till the murmuring temple
Holds only happily pair'd ladies with knights.
Tinkle, tinkle the bells, the music riseth,
To its voluptuous onwardings all move ;
The pairs commingling not, yet all together
Beneath the golden roof, around the altar,
Around the ivy-crown'd illuminate statues

Of leaping bacchanals,—they move, they dance.
Longer and louder the arising music
Utters its challenges ; in dizzy pleasure
Each lady smiles divine, with swimming eye,
And head fall'n backward, whilst her partner gazing
Down in her flushing countenance, whirls her on.
They pause ; the ladies on their worshipping knights
Lean kind.   Now float amongst them gentlest sounds,
Confusing, folding them ; with liquid light
O'erfilling their eyes ; and teaching every voice
Yet gentler lingering ; wreathing round each pair
Deliberate 'prisoning strains, resistlessly,
Yet fondly binding them :—the music dies ;
Silence possesses the temple ; amber dusk
Fills it from roof to pavement, and therein
The revellers rest.   Anon the wilful queens
Feign weariness of love-toying, and again
Entreat to dance.   Now how the minstrels bend
And riot in their task ; the merciless music
Sweeps eddying on, and on each lady whirls,
And whirling aloft her draperies, her limbs
Startle the hall with symmetry, like sea-surge
The light lace heap'd above each shelterless knee.
The merciless music gives no moment's respite,
Urging all action it sweeps out all thought,
Its secret hurrying notes bewilder sense,

Utterly falleth on her lover's bosom
Each eye-closed lady ; with a cry of joy,
Her lover takes her.

                From the temple's altar,
Now steps the Empress of this festival ;
The peerless maiden, round whose crowned beauty
Delay'd the dancing, while the dancers worshipp'd
The inscrutable splendour of her lofty brow
As over all she smiled ; she steps unnoticed,
And all smile vanishes from her downcast face :
Hastily she quits her kingdom, and alone
Threads with impatient steps the winding paths
Of many gardens, till she reach the place
Of an acacia, 'neath whose pendant branches
That suffering lily smiles.
Why is thy lifted gaze so discontent,
Beautiful maiden ? yon majestic moon,
Proud bursting through the gathering clouds of night,
As a frigate through a storm-toss'd sea—yon stars,
Happy resplendently—yon caves of azure,
Nor storm, nor wind, can near—have these no power
To calm the trouble of thy countenance
To fearless reverence, to assure thy soul
To comforting love ? Wherefore, oh gentlest one,

Dost throw thyself in passionate disquiet
Wild to the ground, scaring the woodland nymphs ?
Oh! why repulse yon sky? The moonlight pains her;—
Uprising, close unto the tree she shrinks,—
Its trunk supports her ; whitely droops her face :
The universe is the millstone round her neck ;
And she cannot lift her eyes.   Anon, her voice,—
Now scarcely heard, as from an outspent struggler,
Now loud with passionate protest, now broken
With powerless pity, utters—
" Eldest of Deities ! beneath whose reign
Trembled no sense ; when motionless, and calm,
All worlds were still, unquivering with pain
Of central fire.; when no ocean roll'd
Her serpent form in continent-strangling folds
Around the struggling earth, thus torture-claspt,
Compell'd to toil its endless orbit round,
The jaws of its still tightening enemy
Plunged deep into its heart ; when no false spring
Summon'd out flowers to feel the sunshine sweet,
And then with freezing rains and venomous blights
Mocking their joy,—over the delicate petals
Of azure and pink blossoms, over leaves
Shrinkingly sensitive and verdant, sending
Filthily crawling insects endlessly,
As a loathsome slow-dragg'd sheet; when human things

Existed not by momentary stops
In their monotonous suffering almost cheated
To acknowledge life not torture, not a rack,
Relaxing now and then its furious tension
To hold alive its victims ; when did never,
Love—by his voice whose passionate affection
Doth wondrously caress, and by the joy
Serene and serious in his face and eye
Apparently enfeatured,—win swift entrance
To each deluded heart, where, once received,
He gradually withdraws his beauteous veil,
In base and hideous buffoonery,
To laugh, to rage, to soil ; when cruellest Hope
Never did rouse and aggravate Desire
By promising displays and amorous movements,
In rapturous happiness to pursue him even
To a bridal couch, that there he close may bind her,
And unpossess'd, spring from her pinion'd limbs,
Mocking her burning agony ; when never
Was trampling passion, or unresting torpor,
Or conflict, or decay :—
By thy remissness in permitting life
To violate this deep tranquillity ;
Creating lidless eyes, to roll, but close not,
'Neath skies of fiery brightness ; forming hearts
As delicate as spring's youngest flower-cup

That thirsteth for the purest dew, to fill them
Up to the very brim with leprous filth ;
By all that I have suffer'd, agonies
Which in the cells of memory are not dead,
But whom I dare not summon, even to witness
In this great need ;—Oh ! by this very fear,—
I dare not look behind, and all before
Makes my soul sick, the present tramples me,
I cannot stay, I cannot on, nor back—
By all this horror, save me :—Hear ! oh Death !
Rouse from thy rest, and hear me, save me, save me,
Mightiest of gods !   Oh ! save !
I plead not ignorant, I not thee deem
The portal guardian of some paradise ;
I seek no paradise, I seek no heaven,
I want forgetfulness, I want but rest,
I want but not to be.   Shall I endure
Resistless years of slavery to life,
And when too torture-spent to feel his malice,
Then cease ?   Oh ! let me in my tyrant's presence
Now tell him he is baffled, bare my limbs
To his vile gaze, and scorn him with this glory,
' Thine never more.'   God, thou dost hear me ! Ha !
I shall feel my limbs, as I forsake my couch,
Weakening, and weakening ; up against the sun
I shall hold my trembling fingers, and perceive

Increasing thinness ; when men talk to me
About the future, shall I be very silent
And inwardly smile.   Oh ! could one die for all !
Or I be alone life-tortured ! millions live ;
I am released, the rack remains, the tyrant
Smileth immortal ;—over those I have loved
His cold eye rolleth.   Heard I now a noise,
Not from the sea, and not from cloud, and not
From centre or surface of the earth, but far,
Farther than science telleth, gather and roll
Of evident destruction ;—saw I now
Blackness sweep out the stars, and yonder moon
Shake like a vessel struck by opposite seas,
Drop down precipitately, and suddenly stay'd,
Turn a dead face amidst the scurrying clouds
As a drown'd man on the waves :—oh, then! oh, then!
While this tight globe did split, the madden'd ocean
Like a great white steed upleaping into heaven
Its death-leap, as mown grass the forests falling ;
The voice of an universal cry proclaiming
All life at once withdrawn ;—
Suddenly would my soul befit its death-time
By wonderful growth, and suffer mightiest thoughts
Of the glory of its storm ;—the stricken world
Grinding its atmosphere to thundering surf
As wild it plunges :—with enormous joy,

Feeling myself last-life, I'd hear all cease ;
And when the air grew icy, when the darkness
Abolish'd vision, into the deepening silence
Would I expire."

        From her whitening face
Now starts its lustre ; closed her quivering lips ;
Fall'n to the ground by passion, she lies paler
Than the lily at her side !   Now, suddenly,
Trembled the moonlight from the gardens ; swiftly,
Clouds swept before the moon ; a swift cold wind
Came, bending all the trees ;—she shudder'd, dead :—
In her dark scatter'd hair the wind-snapt lily
Lay with its lifeless leaves ; from its bare roots
Fierce sneak'd their worm.   Oh, friends ! what secret
   woe
Had blooded the vision of this pagan lady,
That she saw nought but wounded suffering
In our glad world !   Children of earth ! believe,
Though but a moth-flight distant yonder temple,
It was no chance that led the lady suffering
To impart her fate to a like suffering flower ;
For it may make sacred every nook in space,
May annihilate despair, alleviate sorrow,
To believe in a rule unseen.

SONG OF THE KINGS OF GOLD.

OURS all are marble halls,
Amid untrodden groves,
Where music ever calls,
Where faintest perfume roves ;
And thousands toiling moan,
That gorgeous robes may fold
The haughty forms alone
Of us—the Kings of Gold.

(Chorus.)   We cannot count our slaves,
Nothing bounds our sway,
Our will destroys and saves,
We let, we create, we slay.
Ha ! ha ! who are Gods ?

E 2

Purple, and crimson, and blue,
Jewels, and silks, and pearl,
All splendours of form and hue,
Our charm'd existence furl ;
When dared shadow dim
The glow in our winecups roll'd ?
When droop'd the banquet-hymn
Raised for the Kings of Gold ?

(*Chorus.*)   We cannot count our slaves,
Nothing bounds our sway,
Our will destroys and saves,
We let, we create, we slay.
     Ha ! ha ! who are Gods ?

The earth, the earth, is ours !
Its corn, its fruits, its wine,
Its sun, its rain, its flowers,
Ours, all, all !—cannot shine
One sunlight ray, but where
Our mighty titles hold ;
Wherever life is, there
Possess the Kings of Gold.

(*Chorus.*)   We cannot count our slaves,

Nothing bounds our sway,
Our will destroys and saves,
We let, we create, we slay.
  Ha ! ha ! who are Gods ?

And all on earth that lives,
Woman, and man, and child,
Us trembling homage gives ;
Aye trampled, sport-defiled,
None dareth raise one frown,
Or slightest questioning hold ;
Our scorn but strikes them down
To adore the Kings of Gold.

(Chorus.) We cannot count our slaves,
  Nothing bounds our sway,
  Our will destroys and saves,
  We let, we create, we slay.
    Ha ! ha ! who are Gods ?

On beds of azure down,
In halls of torturing light,
Our poison'd harlots moan,
And burning toss to sight ;

They are ours—for us they burn;
They are ours, to reject, to hold;
We taste—we exult—we spurn—
For we are the Kings of Gold.

(Chorus.)   We cannot count our slaves,
Nothing bounds our sway,
Our will destroys and saves,
We let, we create, we slay.
Ha! ha! who are Gods?

The father writhes a smile,
As we seize his red-lipp'd girl,
His white-loin'd wife; aye, while
Fierce millions burn, to hurl
Rocks on our regal brows,
Knives in our hearts to hold—
They pale, prepare them bows
At the step of the Kings of Gold.

(Chorus.)   We cannot count our slaves,
Nothing bounds our sway,
Our will destroys and saves,
We let, we create, we slay.
Ha! ha! who are Gods?

In a glorious sea of hate,
Eternal rocks we stand ;
Our joy is our lonely state,
And our trust, our own right hand ;
We frown, and nations shrink ;
They curse, but our swords are old ;
And the wine of their rage deep drink
The dauntless Kings of Gold.

(Chorus.)   We cannot count our slaves,
Nothing bounds our sway,
Our will destroys and saves,
We let, we create, we slay.
Ha ! ha ! who are Gods ?

THE MASQUERADE DRESS.

THE hall of the dancers with light was ablaze;
But for Cressida's presence the dancing delays;
She, alone in her chamber, was sheathing her limbs
In soft silk, that display'd all their forms and their
    whims;
O'er her body the same silk she brought with gay
    scorn,
For the rind fits its fruit as this silk-sheath was worn.

Beautiful did she stand; pearl-hued was the vest;
To her waist, by degrees, its rich colours increased;
To her feet, from her waist, by degrees they did fade,
And her limbs seem'd all light in their faint mas-
    querade;
Like a young rose-bud's cup, towards her neck it did
    close;
Tis the garb of a boy; her breasts underneath rose.

The dance-music sounded; she laugh'd a boy's laugh;
And she shook her gay curls down a foot and a half;
Then she narrow'd her waist with a girl's waist-band,
And smilingly strove with a boy's stride to stand:
In a girl's gentle slippers she slipp'd her small feet,
And she sprang towards the hall singing loudly and
    sweet.

" Who cares for the grape till his throat be dry ?
Who blesses the stream till the sun rides high ?
What man to his mistress will fitly complain
Till she sport with his love, and increase it to pain ?
I'll lure him, repel him, repel while I lure;
For the wilder its passion, the dearer its cure.

" Love's a chase, and I'll fly; 'tis the flying invites;
A thing nearly lost shows tenfold its delights;
Should chance dare dishevel my robes as I'm flown,
Why, I'll turn to tread down the pert chance, and be
    shown.
Tush ! what though the vision my huntsman inflame,
The more ardent the hunting, the dearer the game.

"Should he flag in the chase, I shall happen to fall;
And prostrate, and helpless, his name I shall call:
He will lift me—he'll trick to caress me the while;
And I'll be too faint quite to note the fond guile.
Tush! what though the burthen his love makes to
　　burn,
The fondlier he'll pray me to hold him in turn.

"Should prudes blame my dress, oh! all beautiful
　　braid,
Yellow, crimson, and green over it shall be play'd;
Like snakes on their sunny banks, soft it shall wind,
Everywhere where a place it can fancy or find;
I'll not feign one repulse, but right onward I'll lure,
Laughing out to my lover,—love makes its own cure!"

REMEMBRANCE OF FEELINGS.

OH ! never may the heart regain
Past feelings, as the mind may thought ;
Departed joy leaves dreariest pain,
But memory of its nature !—nought :
Then cease remembrance to reprove ;
I shall forget, alas ! too soon
Not that you gave me leave to love,
But what the heaven that was that boon.

I shall forget,—nay ! World's alone !
I shall remember, with dark fear,
With mean disgust at all that's known,
With self-despair's most lying sneer,—
That this life loved you, and that their
Its ramifications shot through heaven ;

And thrill'd with measureless rapture, when
Thereby heaven's bliss to you seem'd driven.

I shall remember I was pure;
Fearlessly loving, ever, the whole;
Sure that eternity's obscure,
All paradised bright stars did roll,
That bearing you, there I might soar,
The joy in your cheek still wildly eyeing,
Its happiness light yet deepening more,
The more my strength rose, heaven defying.

I shall remember each love-scene,
From love's first dawn to this wild end;
Your deepening clasp, your rapturous mien,
The murmuring sounds your heart did send;—
Take, take his jewels from your brow;
Bend, if your heart be not cold stone;
And I will whisper to you now
What the forgettings that I moan.

I shall forget what was that heaven,
Through which my loving life did spread;

I shall forget the bliss me given,
When it seem'd you through that heaven I led;
I shall forget how feel the pure,
Though remembering their bliss divine ;
How pulsed the life yours did immure,
Though remembering that life was mine.

And these forgetting, all beside
In life will darken deepening gloom ;
The world of these deprived, denied,
Will seem to surge, a reeking tomb ;
Such darkness may be truth, but when
We loved, how different dream'd this heart ;
Might I recall love's feelings, then
Perchance the dream might not depart.

Then cease remembering to reprove ;
I shall forget, alas ! too soon,
Not that you gave me leave to love,
But what the heaven that was that boon.
Would, lady ! that the heart could gain
Past feelings, as the mind may thought ;
The hours might then give up their pain,
And be with memoried raptures fraught.

ODE TO THOUGHT.*

WHETHER you make futurity your home,
    Spirits of thought !
Or past eternity ;—come to me, come !
    For you have long been sought :
I've look'd to meet you in the morning's dawn,
    Often, in vain ;
I've follow'd to her haunts the wild young fawn ;
    Through sunshine, and through rain,
I have waited long and fondly ; surely you will come,
Familiarly as doves returning to their home.

Oh ! I have need of you ; if you forsake
    My troubled mind,
Whence can it strength and consolation take,
    Or peace or pleasure find ?
For the great sake of the eternal spring
    Of all your might,—

* This poem originally appeared in Tait's *Edinburgh Magazine*, September 1838, pp. 581-582.—ED.

Unto me desolate, some comfort bring ;
    Unto me dark, some light :
Come crowdingly, and swift, that I may see
Upon your wings their native radiancy.

I know that ye must have a glorious dwelling :—
    Whether it rise
Past mortal ken, where the old winds are swelling
    Choired cries ;*
Whether, like eagles, on some lunar mountain
    Ye fold your wings,
Or sport beside that rosy and tranquil fountain,
    Whence daylight springs ; †
I know your home is beautiful ; and this belief
Brings glowing sunshine thro' the cloudiness of grief.

Come not with soften'd utterance of the song, ‡
    That gushes in your land ;
But as ye hear it, undisturb'd, and strong,
    Pour it where now I stand ;

* " Unbroken harmonies " is the reading of 1838.—Ed.
† Or sport beside that clear and tranquil fountain,
    Whence rosy daylight springs.—1838.
‡ Bring not the soften'd echoes of the song—*ib.*

A glorious echo these hanging cliffs shall roll
    O'er this great sea;
However far it speed, shall speed my soul
    Thrice lifed with glee;*
Will it not lead where I may clearly see
Countries whose law is love, whose custom, liberty! †

There is a noise within this tranquil heaven!
    This ocean has a voice!
Through these tall trees a mighty tone is driven,
    That bids me to rejoice.
In the clear greenness of these tumbling waters
    I see a face,
Exceeding far in beauty man's pale daughters!
    Bright and unwavering grace
Sits round its brows, proclaiming heavenly glory;
Around it leap the waves, roaring to whiteness hoary. ‡

---

  * These hanging cliffs shall make a rolling echo
      With this great sea;
    However far it float, my soul shall follow,
      Mad with its melody.—1838.

  † love and peaceful liberty?—*ib.*

  ‡ Exceeding far the look of man's pale daughters—
      Bright, undescriptive grace
    Breaks from the brow, proclaiming heavenly glory,
    Lighting the waves with foam and whiteness hoary.—*ib.*

Ye come ! ye come ! like stars down the dark night,
    Boldly leaping !
I hear the mighty rushing of your flight,
    Loud music sweeping.
The unconceived splendour of your speed
    Is not more great
Than the oceanic choirings that precede
    And tide your state ;
Fill me with strength to bear, and power to tell
The wonders gathering round, that man may love me
      well.*

---

* Than the songs intermingled, that exceed
    All Nature can create.
Fill me with strength, that I may nobly tell
The wonders of your speech, that men may love me well.
          1838.

EARLY SPRING.

I ALWAYS roved the woodlands o'er
   In the early time of spring;
But never had discern'd before
   What seeing now I sing:
So faileth oft the soul to see
   The beauty round it rife,
That none may think how sweet would be
   Perfectly-vision'd life.

No young green leaves bedeck'd the trees,
   Only the thrush did sing,
And his song rose not, but did steal,
   Timidly whispering;
No flowers did paint the wind-swept meads,
   No fragrance skimm'd the air;

The sunshine on the ponds shone cold,—
   Cold were the paths and bare.

But the sky was blue with its own soft blue,
   And the sunshine pierced the wind,
And would cling to the trunks of the forest kings,
   Where the shivering primrose pined :
And there was not a cloud to mar the hope
   That shone in the soft blue sky ;
And the air was so clear that the wrinkles of care
   Were smiled away from the eye.

When, gazing round me, gentlest rest
   Into my soul did flow ;
Such rest as summer evening sends,
   When labourers homeward go ;
I knew not whence this rest could come,—
   The air was busy and bright,
And the forest torrent raged along,
   Heavily rolling white.

I laid beneath an ancient elm,
   Vex'd to be made the slave

Of influence I could not see,
　　Or appropriate, or outbrave ;
But as mine eyes did read the boughs
　　Countlessly o'er me wove,
There came to me even gentler rest,
　　And then no more I strove ;

But passive lay, till I surmised
　　'Twas the tree that gave the rest ;
And I sent my gaze through all his boughs
　　With loving and trusting quest :
No leaves were wing'd, its sprigs and stems,
　　Countlessly many, I saw ;
They all did flourish different-wise,
　　Yet none did apart withdraw.

And I noticed they all were rounded soft,
　　And feather'd with buds of down ;
And though hued with the hue of juicy life,
　　Richly and greenishly brown,
That these multitudinous varying boughs,
　　Unteased with leaves slept still ;
Hence cometh my rest, I cried, and rose,
　　And gazed at each tree-clad hill.

And in bold relief against the sky,
   Everywhere round me, rose
Innumerably, these leafless trees ;
   And I saw the deep repose—
Not a torpid sleep, but a living rest—
   In their soft and nervelike boughs,
Spread betwixt me and that azure heaven,
   Whose lustre such vision allows.

And now I maintain that the earliest spring,
   Though boasting no scarlet or green,
Hath its own peculiar beauteousness,
   In the leafless and moveless treen ;
Whose branches sleep in the golden air,
   Passively bearing its tide ;
Soft with the down of a thousand buds,
   Unitedly branching wide.

THE GEM OF COQUETTES.

A song ! a song ! Kate, a song !
To your spirited stomacher sure must belong !
    Curving out,
    With pertinent pout,
The most exquisite orb in creation above ;
    Displaying the grace
    Of each neighbouring place,
And the forms of the limbs that beneath him move ;
    Oh ! why seem severe ?
    Why, why should you fear
Your stomacher's history, mistress, to hear ?

    You gave him his place, and taught him to ride,
Soon after you from your bed did slide ;—
    From bosom to knee,
    So unreasonably, -

Your shape was veil'd, that the glass did frown,
 And so you took
 With your wickedest look,
This gem of coquettes, and bound him down,
 To wanton and pout,
 And show you out,
And make all your lovers grow very devout.

 And truly with all the most gallant of airs,
Through the parlours he rides you, he rides you up-
 stairs,
 Seeming to say,—
 Here I'm order'd to stay,
The underneath beauty to guard and invest;—
 While slily he shows
 How each moment that flows
That beauty against him swells scornful protest;
 And well though he knows
 How his tricks expose,
With exquisite insolence on he goes.

 A truce ! a truce ! mistress, a truce !
In a moment this history I will reduce,
 If you'll let me kneel,

And gently steal
From this gem of coquettes a devotional kiss ;—
    Else I follow him still,
    Till at midnight's thrill
You bid him good-bye ; and much more than this
    Will I boldly relate,
    And with song celebrate,
Of him and his fellows too, beautiful Kate.

A DEVELOPMENT OF IDIOTCY.

FEARFUL the chamber's quiet; the veil'd windows
Admit no breath of the out-door throbbing sunshine;
She moans in the bed's dusk;—some sharp revulsion
Shuddereth her lips as though she strives to cry,
But finds no voice : she draweth up her limbs,
They flutter fast and shake their covering.
Seven watch her, as might men a noonday sun,
Who vanishing backward in the top of heaven,
Leaves them all blindly staring through the dark;—
Physicians and servitors;—pryingly they bend,
While by her head kneels one in agony.
A gloom seems passing o'er her countenance,
As the shadow of a cloud across a field;
Perchance the ghastly expression of the horror
With which life ends : it darken'd but a moment;
Now she turns white as stone, as fix'd, as dead.
God ! ten days hence she laugh'd out in thy sunshine!
Her filmed eyes look'd, gestured happiness !—
They have no look at all.

The seven shuffle from the bed which hides
Her clutching fingers, and her doubled limbs,
So stiffening 'twixt its sheets; and one by one,
They coweringly glance towards her fall'n mouth,
And all together hurry from out the room,
Not caring to leave it singly.   All is still;
He rises from the ground, fast locks the door,
Breaks through her couch-clothes, feels about her
        heart;—
All there is motionless: he lifts her hand;—
There is nothing but dead form, it moves not, warms
        not,
It weighs, it slides away, it drops like lead,
Lies where it dropp'd: recoiling, the man gasps,
As though by ocean seized: his jaws contract,
He bounds, he rends the window; savagely
Looking right up into the broad blue sky,
No congruous curses aid him,—he is silent,
Save with his clenched hands, his writhing face,
His heaving chest.

            He was a force-fill'd man,
Whom the wise envy not; his passionate soul,
Being mighty to detect life's secret beauty,
Detecting, would display; and in his youth,

When first bright visions unveil'd before his gaze
Their moral loveliness and physical grace,
With the sweet melody of affectionate clamour
He sang them to the world, and bade it worship :
But the world unrecognized his visions of goodness,
Or recognizing, hated them and him.
As some full cloud foregoes his native country
Of sublime hills, where bask'd he near to heaven,
And descends gently on his shadowy wings
Through the hot sunshine to refresh all creatures ;
So came he to the world ;—as the same cloud
Might slowly wend back to his Alpine home,
Unwatering the plain,—so left he men
Who knew not of their loss.

Yet sad was loneliness, and never beheld he
Aught beautiful amidst our world of beauty—
From sunsets flushing heaven with sudden crimson,
To the moth's wing that spots the poplar leaf ;
Never develop'd he fact, or dream'd he glory,
Without being faint for sympathy,—that one
Might share with him his blissful adoration,
Loving even as he loved.   This holy want
Wasted him unto sickness : then she came ;
And while he hung above death's gloomy gulf,

Sternly considering its maddening stillness,
Measuring the plunge ;—her soft voice call'd to him :
He turn'd ; he saw her eyes his soul acquiring ;
He saw her look of woman's infinite giving ;
He saw her arms of eloquent entreaty,
Praying indeed to clasp him : yea, she saved ;
And oh ! but he was happy, for her being
Loved all things as he loved, and thence to him
Came hope and rapturous quiet.   Then, no more
Lamented he the wingless minds of men,
Than pines the swan, who down the midnight river
Moves on considering the reflected stars,
Because dark reptiles burrowing in the ooze
Care not for starry glories.

She is dead within that bed ; and never more
Will she hearken to his dreams of paradise,
And wind her arms around him, sweetly paling
With excess of happiness.   .

Three days and nights he haunted a near mountain ;
The sky was cloudless, and the sunshine strong,
And not one mournful breeze ever stole to him,
Loosening his tears.   High on its top he stood ;

His voice rose solemn, and loud, and fearlessly :—
The angels watching him midway in the air,
Rush'd swift to heaven, and all heaven's shining group
Weepingly pleaded against his blasphemy ;—
"Roll back ! thou lying robe of halcyon blue !
And let me speak unto thy cowering Lord,
The slayer of my love, that I may tell him
My infinite hate, that he may slaughter me :
He has killed her : I will not have his life ;—
Thou lying robe of halcyon blue, roll back !"
The peaks prolong'd with echoings his defiance ;
Still the sky stirr'd not—still the sunshine smiled,
And beneath the smile low rose a low wild sound :—
"And then my breast will be as cold as hers,—
My face as white—as signless."

The fourth day, backed he rush'd into the chamber,
Where she lay coffin'd.   None dared speak to him ;
Great grief is majesty ; he is alone.
Oh ! is that she, or can it all be dreaming ?
Fine lace is plaited round her countenance ;
Her eyes are closed, as they would seem to say,
"My last farewell is taken."   Round her lips
Is fixed a sweet smile ; her shrunken hands
Are clasp'd upon her bosom, their dark fingers

Cunningly hidden.   Can it all be dreaming ?
Striving to stare the mistiness from his eyes,
Griping his throat, he lightly presses her hand,—
The pressure of his fingers doth not vanish ;—
Senseless he falls.

This singer of the beautiful, who retreated
Back from a scowling world ; this force-fill'd man,
Who finding nothing whereunto he might sing,
Of power unutter'd, and of passion unshared,
Nigh died ; this gentle minister of love,
Who, hail'd by loving sympathy, thrice lived
In singing his deities, and seeing them loved,
And loving their lover, and forgetting all else ;—
Is now a thing that hideth most fair weathers,
Outwandering in most glooms,—after whose path
The village boys shout " idiot," that some sport
His face may make them, when it turns enraged
With idiot rage, that slinks to empty smiles,
And tears, and laughter, empty.   His chief habit
Is secretly rending piecemeal beauteous flowers ;—
He ever shows when the groaning thunder toils,
And when the lightnings flash ! and they who meet
His shrinking, shuddering, blank countenance,
Wonder to heaven with somewhat shaken trust.

YOUTH'S DEPARTURE.

OH ! all the bliss of youth must end,
 His boundless trust, his fancied home,
His noble instinct to expend
 His heart away where'er he roam ;
Even Nature's face will take his gaze,
 And glance him back no thrill ;
He'll wander down life's thousand ways,
 And be a wanderer still.

This is his doom !—to look around
 With eyes unused to gloom,
And find no splendour deck the ground,
 No song, no scent, no bloom :
This is his doom !—to watch decaying,
 As soon as it dawns, the light ;
To follow the morning, bravely straying,
 And meet with a dreary night.

And thus to see your youth departing,
   Is to watch your chain clench'd on ;
Blow after blow fresh anguish darting ;—
   Oh ! when will youth be gone !
'Tis to find yourself all lonely leaving
   A friend-o'ercrowded shore
In a wizard barque whose rudderless heaving
   Will waft you back no more.

HIGH SUMMER.

I NEVER wholly feel that summer is high,
However green the trees, or loud the birds,
However movelessly eye-winking herds
Stand in field ponds, or under large trees lie,
Till I do climb all cultured pastures by,
That hedged by hedgerows studiously fretted trim,
Smile like a lady's face with lace laced prim,
And on some moor or hill that seeks the sky
Lonely and nakedly,—utterly lie down,
And feel the sunshine throbbing on body and limb,
My drowsy brain in pleasant drunkenness swim,
Each rising thought sink back and dreamily drown,
Smiles creep o'er my face, and smother my lips, and
   cloy,
Each muscle sink to itself, and separately enjoy.

G

A HAPPY SADNESS.

One smile is all thy brow, love,
  Thine eyes are all delight ;
And many a sprite I trow, love,
  Watches thee through the night ;
But though thy brow and eyes
  With deep delight are glad,
Though most thy joy I prize,
  Yet I am sad.

I joy to watch thy brow, love,
  When not toward me its sky ;
When glorious thought, as now, love,
  Bright riots in thine eye ;
But when thy steadfast gaze
  Of love o'erfills my heart,
No answering glance I raise,
  But tears will start.

Oh ! do not read my sigh, love,
  As if it languaged woe ;

In silence I would die, love,
   Ere woe to thee I'd show ;
Nor deem that I repine
   Intenser love to wring ;
As heaven is earth's thou'rt mine ;—
   Yet tears will spring.

For I can never speak, love,
   One half the faith I feel ;
And song is all too weak, love,
   My passion to reveal ;
And music hath no measure,
   In nature nought can be,
To sign how vast the treasure,—
   Thy love to me.

And how canst thou believe, love,
   The love I cannot speak ;
And sometimes may'st thou grieve, love,
   To think my passion weak ;
Oh ! heaven-soul'd, well I heed
   Heaven's love should'st thou have had ;
Mine's heaven's, but cannot plead,
   And I am sad.

HARDINESS OF LOVE.

Oh ! Love is a hardy flower,
That anywhere will blow,
In sunshine or in shower,
In happiness or woe :—
A lady, sitting lone,
Was very sadly singing ;
" No hope pervades my moan,
Despair my heart is wringing ;
I lured him from the side
Of one who loved him well ;
And now a maniac bride
She fills a maniac's cell ;
He sought my love for peace,
And when it could not be,
His prayers did wildly cease,
He died in pardoning me."

Oh ! Love is a hardy flower,
That anywhere will blow,
In sunshine or in shower,
In happiness or woe :—
A youth was passing by,
And heard this lady's strain,
And answer'd, "Guiltier I,
Would death would end my pain ;
A girl had made her heart
A glorious throne for me,
From all she did depart,
And brought to me its key ;
I loved her not, I took,
And I did coldly prey ;
Then drave her with my look
To mart her charms away."

Oh ! Love is a hardy flower,
And anywhere will blow,
In sunshine or in shower,
In happiness or woe :—
To the lady's eyes did look
The youth's, with pity dim ;
And when her hand he took,
She look'd the same to him ;

Her cheek to his he press'd,
Their forms together fell,
And though they wept,—the rest
'Twere very vain to tell ;—
For Love is a hardy flower,
That anywhere will blow,
In sunshine or in shower,
In happiness or woe.

A SLAVE'S TRIUMPH.

"DEATH to the aristocrats !" the people roar'd,—
Death to my master—each man fiercely thought,—
As through the capital of France they pour'd,
A revolution's mob, with madness fraught:
Before a stately building paused one band ;
Awhile its leader bade them there abide ;
And where his Lord and his Lord's kindred stand,
　　　　　He sprang and cried—

" Where is your scorn ! where is the insolent eye,
Narrowing its lids to look at me ; where, where,
The averted face that seemed wrench'd awry,
Sick at my presence, that ye yet did bear,
Even to enslave me ! seem thus sick once more !
With narrowing eyes now speak me your decree !
For beneath your palace human tigers roar !
　　　　　I hold the key !

" You merciless wretches ! what ! you kneel, you whine,
To smile to me you dare ! one smile again,
And the mob is rending ye :—rise, masters mine !
I'll give you a boon to see your old disdain ;
To hear your words slow, insolent, as of yore
Chuckle at the shame they knew they burn'd through
    me ;
For beneath your palace human tigers roar !
                I hold the key !

"God ! how they hate me ! this, this, this, is life !
Aha ! white fiends ! I am merciless ! one hour
Ago, and ye might have slain me with the knife,
When 'neath your whips my flesh did shrink and
    cower !
Had ye but known when to slay me ye forbore,
How I drank your blood, while I for life did plea !
For the tigers are starved that underneath you roar !
            And I hold the key !

" Can you not tell these avengers of my shame
How I loathe, despise them ;—ye were saved, saved,
    saved !

The beasts have lick'd your feet, and again would
    tame !
Aha ! they will sword you when this hand is waved !
They will wrench your hearts out ! stumble in your
    gore !
Can you not speak them ! beasts they are like ye !
But mine, mine, mine ! for you they rage and roar !
           I hold the key !"

INACTIVITY.

On such a day as this, when songs of birds,
Floating through wide-flung windows, upon breezes
Woodbine and clover-scented, gently trouble
The happy and basking spirit to desires
For yet more happiness; when the rich hedges
Sleep on the fields so still and sunnily
That housemen long to go and lie beside them,
In their long grass hay-dry and poppy-throng'd,
To make companions of the grasshoppers,
And sleepily dream towards the insect motives
Impelling their quick leaps;—who has not taken
His country staff, unto the household saying,
"I go to seek if of the flowers of spring,
One violet be left," and quietly stroll'd
Lonesomely out unto the fields and trees,
Entering upon the broad brown waving meadows,
As a seafowl giving herself unto the sea,
When its waves are calm; and then beneath some
    hedge,
Yieldingly lain himself in pleasant languor:
Letting his head fall deep amidst the hay,

His eyelids shutting out the external world,
His mind considering nothing, pleasantly powerless;
Or if perchance a stray thought steals to it,
'Tis of its own tranquillity.

The sunshine of this summer afternoon
Not in my parlour enter'd; but abroad
Copiously as ever it everywhere dwelt;
Surrendering itself up unto each tree,
To be spill'd about on all the leaves and twigs,
Sleeping in all the secret crevices
Of the rich rose; broad o'er the sweeping hills,
The swelling meadows and the spangled gardens,
Benignantly outspread. I gazed, and gazed;
I gave a moment to encase my books,
And I was in the sunshine, and my blood
Sprang at its greeting. I was in the fields,
And up around me sprang the larks like rockets
On a jubilee day:—a bank of sand surmounting,
I stepp'd into a wood, with pleasant care,
Opening the twining branches, that imposed
Desirable hindrance: angrily scream'd
A swiftly darting throstle on before me;
Two bees adown the narrow pathway flew,
And a bewilder'd butterfly; I stay'd

To joy in the delicious noise of leaves,
In the fresh earthy smells ;—I wander'd on
Past the slow-pacing pheasant, and the jay,
Who would not let me leave him, but still follow'd
With his harsh scream.　And now I reach'd an
　　opening,
A short-turf'd lawn, that fenced by silvery stems
Of circling beeches, seem'd a quiet home.
I enter'd ; flowingly between the trees
Floated the blackbird's strains ; they paused, I paused ;
Raising in sympathy to the tranquil heaven
My tranquil thought ; like a great eye it shone,
It seem'd to bend in love ; I gazed, and gazed ;
Its look sank nearer me ; I gasp'd, I fell,
Panting to be embraced up by the heaven,
As virgin womanhood for love's caress ;
My soul close clung to that far-stretching glory,
'Neath which I reel'd ; it stretch'd there undisturb'd
By tower or boundary, and my tranced spirit
Passively drank in its elysian calm.
Oh, blue, blue sky ! oh fathomlessly blue sky !
Your motionless band of silvery cloudlets,
Like white swans sleeping on a windless lake,
In happy undesiring repose,—were not
More compass'd by you, more retired within you,
Than I, in that blest time ; nor wish, nor thought,

Nor hope, nor grief, found room within my being,
Fill'd with your beautiful presence.

Within the sanctuary of these circling trees,
Thus lay I, slave to the sky; when a white deer
Noiselessly through the intertangled boughs
Did thrust his head; he shrank, and in the forest
Back vanished, most like a silvery cloud.
Retreating, he had shaken on my face
A blown convolvulus; the which upholding
Against the sun, that I might read its veins,
From its recess a crimson-scaled wonder,
A ladybird with richly-spotted wings,
Soar'd through the sunshine.   Now from heaven's
    thraldom
My mind this insect's flight enfranchised;
And being freed to all the things around,
They all impress'd me.   Now I heard the partridge
Make the copse echo with his cheerful crow;
Anon my pulsings seem'd to keep the time
Of the cuckoo's music; in the sun's faint streamings.
I watch'd the twinkling bands of tipsy insects;
I watch'd the sun's gold lustre through the leaves,
Illuminating all their make, descend,
As the breeze swerved them into it for a moment,

Letting them drop again.   A hundred beauties,
Words will not image, throng'd my echoing soul ;
And she from all instinctively did abstract
Their capital feature ; life, a massive lyre,
On my proud thought-directed vision rose,
Swinging within its home of boundlessness,
Singing for ever in an Eternal Breeze,
Of whom this landscape, with its gentle beauty,
Was one soft utterance.

                    A little while
The contemplation of this abstract thought
Possess'd me with content ; but soon there came,
Like a chill wind, a sense of gloominess.
The heavens were blue ; " Yes," sigh'd I, " they are
    blue,
But what of blue ?" the birds continued singing,
But song seem'd nought ; the leaves were green and
    golden ;
" Oh," moaned I, " what good in green or golden,
Or trees, or birds, or skies, or anything ?"
The unity in the boundlessness of life
Gave me no thrill.
Philosophy ! expound me whence this gloom ;
And why, when I had call'd the village cur,

As he rush'd hare-chasing through my lonely glade,
And had made the circles of his eyes grow brighter,
His tail quick wag out with exuberant joy,
His teeth affectionately bite my hand,
By my caresses,—unobserved by me,
The gloomful pain did pass from out my being,
Leaving a tranquil sadness, that but waited
A change of place, to grow to cheerful calm !
Is it that man is all too great, to rest
The passive slave of any heaven or earth,
Of Nature's shows and forces ?   Of a God,
Hath man the causative destiny and essence ?
Must he fulfil such destiny, or find pain ?
And rose within my being this troubling gloom
From passiveness continued ?   Did it pass
While I was making glad the village cur,
Because I commenced to influence ?

                             The hermit
Must have his redbreast to supply with crumbs ;
The dungeon'd captive makes himself of spiders
Things to protect and feed ; the evil man,
To expend his passion to influence, will torture ;
The good man blesses at the same impulsion ;—
But to influence both require.

THE MOURNER'S ISLE.

THE endless rains that gently fall
In Carisbrook Castle Island, dear,
Can soften the mourner's heart, and call
From his burning brain the loosening tear ;
Then voyage with me to that wizard isle,
There longest on earth will sad memories delay ;
Its sunshine is only a softly sad smile,
And its flowers are too tender and brief to be gay.

There will ne'er pain thee jest or joy ;
Its life is as still as its gliding streams ;
And the peasant you meet, and the peasant's boy,
Wend there as if sadly remembering sweet dreams ;
There the herds are all pensive ; the winds all are low ;
By starts the birds warble ; each tree seems a pall ;
And there never despair robs the heart of its woe,
To leave it accursed with cold hatred for all.

When its sadness, its smiles, and its gentle rain
Shall have loosen'd thy tears, away I will flee;
For I know that a friend is a bitter pain,
When a love is gone to eternity:
Oh! retreat to the isle! no more may I pray;
The one who should move thee so, sister, is gone;
But in that wizard isle, still his memory would stay;
And unfound and unseen thou may'st weep there alone.

SONG OF THE GOLD-GETTERS.

"The essence of trade is to buy cheap, and sell dear."—
House of Commons, England, 1843.

OH ! truth may have suited the knights of old,
And have royally crown'd the barbarian's brow;
And the Hottentot's mother his grave may have
    scroll'd
With "He never once lied;" but Utopia now,
In our civilized world, is the only land
Where truth could be worshipp'd, where truth could
    live ;
For from statesman to tradesman all utterance is
    plann'd
Any meanings but true ones to hint at or give.
      Lie ! let us lie ! make the lies fit;
      It's the only way mortals their fortunes can knit.

If the minister orders war-ships at a foe,
He pretends they are bound quite a different way ;

And where is the man that shall dare to throw
Disdain on the lie, or the truth to say ?
The traveller, hearing the lion's roar,
Lies to the lion by feigning death,
And lives by the lie ; and what can there be more
In the minister's lie to the enemy's teeth ?
    Lie ! let us lie ! make the lies fit ;
    It's the only way mortals their fortunes can knit.

"The best policy's honesty," horn-books tell,
Though we know who lies best gets the best of the
    pelf ;—
'Tis the sire for his children the axiom likes well,
For the lie's an advantage he wants all himself ;
For the same cunning reason your pulpits, your
    thrones,
Your senates, your judges the axiom repeat ;
Each wants to monopolise lying, and moans
That he can't with this lie truth from other men
    cheat.
    Lie ! let us lie ! make the lies fit ;
    It's the only way mortals their fortunes can knit.

Truth now starves in garrets, or rots in a gaol,
Whate'er may have been in the times gone by ;

And supremacy national, "cakes and ale,"
Honour and station reward the lie ;
Let us lie then like statesmen, like fathers, and gold
We shall heap and keep ;—the world is war,
And out of war's articles none will uphold
The virtue of truth when a falsehood gains more.

> *(Chorus.)*—Lie ! let us lie ! Oh ! we'll make the
> lies fit ;
> It's the only way mortals their fortunes can knit.

EYEING THE EYES OF ONE'S MISTRESS.

WHEN down the crowded aisle my wandering eyes
'Lighted on thine fix'd scanningly on my face,
They struck not passion fire, but in their place
Did settlingly fix themselves, contemplative-wise,
Thine eyes to fathom ;—for as one that lies
On mountain side where thick-leaved branches vein
'Twixt him and the sun, and gazes o'er the plain
That wide beneath him variedly amplifies ;
I think my being was elevatedly lain
On its own thought, and in thy being gazing
With tranquil speculation, that did gain
Singular delight : thus mine eyes thine appraising,
By dial reckoning, only a moment spent ;
Whole ages by the heart's right measurement.

But when thine eyelids bent into thy gaze
Nearing regard and instigating light ;
Their lashes narrowing o'er the dewy blaze
That suddenly thine eyes did appetite ;

Narrowing as if thou feared'st to invite
Too utterly, but truly that their motion
Caressingly closing faintly, might excite
My tranquil gaze to passionate devotion ;—
Then suddenly seemed I an infinite life ;
Infinitely falling down before thy shrine ;
Infinitely praying thy descent ; the strife
Of the aisle's crowd seem'd gone ; thine eyes and
  mine,
Devouring distance, into each other grew ;
While thine unfeigning lids gloriously upward flew.

REPOSE IN LOVE.

I FLEW to thee, love, I flew to thee, love,
   From a world where all's deceit;
The river rushing to the sea, love,
   Speeds not so wildly fleet:
And now while bask'd beneath thine eyes,
   Where truth so calmly glows,
Than the saint's first rest in Paradise
   I know more sweet repose.

In former times beside thee glowing,
   I've seen all life grow bright;
Kindness o'er hardest faces flowing,
   O'er falsehood new truth-light:
And then I thought it matchless bliss
   To see the stars twice shine,
All baseness from the earth to miss,
   Because I felt me thine.

But now I know joy deeper far
    Attends our love's career;
It now no more veils life's vile war,
    But lifts me past life's sphere;
And no joy may with this compare,—
    I see life's base design,
Yet know no fear, no pain, no care,
    Because I feel me thine.

SONG TO A ROSE.

BEAUTIFUL rose ! a song for thee,
   This shiny month of June ;
Thy red buds brighten every tree,
   And so my soul in tune
Would carol thy beauty, star of the wildwood,
Image and joy of careless childhood !

I strive to sing, but mine eyes grow dim,
   I fray thy leaves away,
And the music sinks to a mournful hymn
   For thy declining day ;
How shall I sing thee, star of the wildwood,
Trembling and sad like advancing childhood !

Slower the melody, slacker the string,
   Thine heart of hearts I have won ;
And the delicate hues of thine innermost ring
   Are stripp'd, and stain'd, and—gone ;

How shall I sing thee, star of the wildwood,
Ravish'd away like the joys of childhood !

Silent the melody, broken the string,—
   Thy light is shed for ever,—
Never more may the shower fresh fragrancy bring,—
   But the spirit would break to *say* " Never ;"
Fiercely I weep, star of the wildwood,
Utterly lost like the joys of childhood !

TO A CORPSE-WATCHER.

EARTH hath no home for thee ! whither wouldst thou ?
Fear'st thou the death-light damping its brow ?
Would'st thou gnash thy wild wrath at the world's
    life-smile,
Or against the unknown blindly howl thy revile ?
Turn thee ! turn thee ! sit by its bed ;
With its hand in thy hand, learn the feel of the dead ;
Think how she yesternight danced down thy hall,
Laughing out gentle light to each melody's call,
Glancing thee girlhood's love, when her fine foot did
    fall
        In the arch feats of dance !

Earth hath no home for thee ! sit by its bed ;
And thy fury will sink when thou feel'st it quite
    dead ;.

For the shadows thou sawest, that rose in its face,
When its mouth shudder'd down into death's fix'd
    grimace,—
The shadows that rose in its face, and therefrom
Came with a shudder,—more blackly shall come
From that same white face in steady succession,
And fill all the room with their soundless procession,
Till thine eye-balls shall start from their swift retro-
    gression,
          Darkening down from the roof.

And the gloom of those shadows shall sink in thy
    brain,
Expelling all thought, and deadening all pain ;
The tide in thy veins shall move heavy and slow,
And the beats of thine heart long-intervall'd go ;
To passionless torpor thy face shall wane,
And omnipotent sleep shall thy life unstrain ;—
By the corpse thou shalt sleep,—by it thou shalt
    wake,
But no glorious rage shall thy nature then shake,
For low idiot tears will thy broken face slake,
          The tears of self-sorrow.

Thou wilt weep; and when wept all thy greatness
  away,
Thou shalt start from the corpse, and its grave-clothes
  array,
And look with no love, but with horror, to its face,
And say that a cold smell doth steam round its place,
The cold smell of corruption;—thou'lt long for the
  day
Of the quick busy world, with its work and its
  play;—
To that day then depart thou,—feel saved in its
  bloom,
Hug thyself with the thought, distant far is thy
  tomb,
Lose thyself in the gay crowds whose bright looks
  assume
All that's most unlike death.

But earth hath no home for thee!—far as thou
  strayest,
Thy heart shall still sneer at all love that thou sayest,
At all love that is said; for thou shalt believe ever
Love to be a false friend, even Death's frown can
  sever;

And thus homeless, and hopeless of home, shalt thou
    mourn,
With bitter life-hate and gnawing self-scorn,
The time when thou thought'st that love could not
    fail so,
The time when such thought from thy damn'd heart
    did go,
That time when above thy slain love there did flow
        Thy tears of self-sorrow.

THE SUICIDE.

LIFE is an island; and eternity's sea
    That girds it round,
Rolleth for ever, vast and gloomily,
    With doubtful sound,
Save when it stormeth up tempestuously,
    Lashing the ground.

Voices are mingled with the rolling waters.
    Unearthly sweet;
They fascinate the island sons and daughters,
    In bands to meet,
And listen, heeding not the wrecks and slaughters
    Roll'd to their feet.

Some walk before this sea with restless wings,
    Strong to dare

The chilling mist its heavy rolling flings ;
 With forehead bare
And flashing brow, resistless genius springs
 Undaunted there.

A naked youth came bounding to its shore,
 Shouting out loud ;
But when he heard the interminable roar,
 His spirit bow'd
One moment, and the next it strove to soar
 Uncheck'd and proud.

Upon his feet and shoulders wings were waving
 Widely and fast ;
Over the quiet country he was leaving
 One look he cast
Of contempt beautiful and godlike craving ;
 Sweet voices pass'd

Out from the sea, towards him richly ringing :
 He hails their tone ;
To explore the deep, the mighty child is winging ;
 Oh ! not alone ;

Concealed sirens toss there wildest singing,
    While golden spray is thrown.

Rushing back came the youth with drooping plume;
    His strength was gone;—
He stands again before the unthridden gloom,
    And still its moan
Wails to him burning melodies that consume
    Him there alone.

His frenzied eye read the eternal ocean;
    His pale lips gave
Echoings to its inscrutable commotion;
    His speech did rave
Language unknown; glancing sublime devotion,
    He pass'd beneath the wave.

I

OPINION'S CHANGE.

The beardless statesman out at monarchy screams,
    " Down trampler by the heel on man's rights, down
    Foe to humanity's universal crown
Because it overdazzles thy false crown's beams ; "—
Thoughtless of human needs, he ever dreams
    Of human " rights ; "—those " rights " being just
        alone
    The singular needs peculiarly his own,—
Such needs as power to test one's own law-schemes :
But learn'd to think, he sees that men, in a king,
    Find much they need,—a thing to which must bow
    Masters as low as serfs ; a man whose brow
Is highest in the state, and yet must spring
Smiles to their smiles ;—and so he lets enjoy
Mankind its many kings, as a child its toy.

A CRISIS.

If when the day was fine, the summer high,
Encentred in this meadow, one revolved
Inquiring gaze, around it he would see
Fencing it, wooden palings, mossy, and mellow'd
To gentle kinds of undecided colour,
By rain and age; then close behind the fence,
All round it rising high, would stop his sight
An impassable verdure of commingled trees,
Offering the eye a thousand fathomless nooks
Fill'd with green dark, but nowhere tunnell'd through
By any passage; 'midst the dark green mass
Would puzzle him fluttering motionings and sounds
—As unassignable as an ant-hill's stir—
Of wild-wood denizens; while frequently
Might song-bird soundlessly from one of its shades
Flit o'er the meadow, and, with closing wings,

Into shade opposite glide ; but from its top
His eye would only lift to a roof of sky.

Within this meadow did no tame thing browse ;
Wild were the hares that canter'd through its ferns ;
Wild were the hawks that wheel'd 'twixt it and
         heaven ;
Its bees were wild bees of some cavernous tree ;
None pluck'd its flowers ; no menial o'er it trod ;
It had been the battle-field, the unsculptured grave,
Of Christian martyrs ; and its reverent lord
Ordain'd it sacred.

The evening church-chimes had dispersed the mowers
From all the fields of toil ; the evening sun
Slanted his golden light, as he did lapse
Towards underneath the earth ; his light was ray'd
So gorgeously upon this sacred meadow,
Its yellow buttercups, its ruby sorrels,
Its milk-white clover, and its cool green grass,
Seem'd blended into one rich colour'd woof,
Changing in hue, as waved beneath the breeze ;—
When leaning therewithin, against its fence,
A light-robed maiden in the whelming sunshine
Exhibited woman symmetry unstirr'd

By womanhood's experience; she lean'd
Fronting the mead; against the lofty fence
Her shoulders settled, and her pertinent feet,*
Pressingly side by side, are forwarded
Into the mead, and planted firmly there;
And from her planted feet to her fall'n back head,
One proud full arch she arches. A large wind
Came o'er the mead, and flaggingly on her fell,
Weighing her vestments downwards and around;
Sleeker than apples show her round young knees;
Show beauteously together twined her limbs :
The frontage of her body broadly orbs;
The sunlight whelmeth all :—loosely her head,
Loosely her neck falls backward; her round chin,
And its rich blood-red lip, now idly sink
Down from the upwardly curved lip above;
While round the corners of her idling mouth,

---

* In the original edition this passage stood thus :—
    When leaned therewithin, against its fence,
    A form white robed, which the whelming sunshine
    Show'd to be fullest symmetry of woman
    Swelling thro' girlhood's prime. Fronting the mead
    She stood; against the fence her shoulders rest;
    Above it gently her head and neck bend back;
    Her long brown hair behind her straightly fall'n
    Leaves unconcealed her twin-breasted bosom,
    Thus raised against her vest; her pertinent feet, &c.

Slow smiling dimples, when her basking eyes,
A little uplifting their nigh-closed lids,
Thrill with voluptuous light,—above her cheeks
Like opening crevices to measureless splendour.
Rounds she out thus on firmly-planted feet
Her enjoying form, and thus her face is naked
In glowing rapture,—because by her stands,
Lovingly gazing on her, he whose gaze
Pours dizzying pleasure over her, to permeate,
Till her shoulders shiver and shrink with her delight.

Feelings, as things, do grow; and growing, change :
The love that bended forth this gazer's face,
Fixing its slightest muscle, and its eyes
Firing to their very depths, had grown and changed.
When first he loved, had risen in him one lusting
Towards her, he had spat into his heart
Intense self-loathing; what was then his love
Words may not scribe, his memory could not seize,
Fancy may compass not; therewith was nought
Of jealousy, or desire, or doubt, or pain;
Nought of self-love, self-consciousness; it join'd
With marvellous adoration, perfectest rest,
Instinctive trust and measureless devotion
And measureless sympathy, but it was not these.

Such in this meadow, by her arch'd-out form,
Was it not now, for it had grown and changed.
'Twas love ! but now every atom of his body
Trembleth for every atom moulding hers ;
'Twas love ! but now he could strangle her from life
Rather than see another bridegroom her ;
Oh ! yes, 'twas love ! for in life's flintiest highways,
He would rush to grovel his being's nakedest bosom
To gain her smile, or cause her one delight.
Yea, still he loved her, utterly ; through the world
Drifting unknown and knowing not ; his mind,
A mirror multiplying a thousand times
Her lonely loveliness,—ever there he gazed,
Still, still she shone ; his will, a trembling rudder,
She held to play with, or to queen ; his body,
Their mutual serf, its separated being,
Never once recognized by any of his thoughts.

Yet never had he spoken to her the love,
Making thus his being with its countless powers,
Her magnificently swift automaton ;
To measureless action spring'd by her in a moment,
To measureless rest subdued.   She saw it, loved it,
Dream'd her world out of it, and yet he fear'd
She knew it not, and knowing, would disapprove.

Now therefore here, into this sacred meadow,
To try her hath he come ; to daringly burst
Into the secretest chambers of her soul,
Its unveil'd moods to see : the talisman
That shall rend away the garments of her being,
All pitilessly nakeding her, he bears ;
He approaches her, he trembles, pales his face,
He would see, yet fears to see.   But even now,
In fond coquetry, or affectionate joy,
She lifts her head ; against the fence behind,
She plants its crown ; her feet move slightly back,
Move back apart and so on tiptoe rising,
Up outwardly she leisurely lifts her form,
The while she talks.   Where now is his intent ?
Thrice his knees bend unconsciously, and thrice
His hand descends towards her lifted heels,
Quivering to fill its hollow with their round.
The struggling eyes of his fire-beflooded face
Devour the unshod archings of her feet,
As he imagineth his caressing mouth
There trampled ; yet around her arching loins
His arms he girds not, but with great control
Apart he stands.   Now suddenly her eyes
Turn'd round to his, their startled lids, once fluttering,
Could not close down, and thus transfix'd, she took
Awhile his rifling glances,—till he moved,

When swift she snatch'd her eyes back, turning pale.
Soon they both feign'd indifference, and spake
Of the meadow sleeping goldenly before,—
The trees around,—the richly-slanting sunlight ;
But as they spake, relapsed with gradual lapse,
Her heels to ground, her shoulders to the fence :
No longer curved she out as a sail wind-fill'd,
For her exquisitely supple body revolved in
Over its ample throne ; and negligently
Her feet slid out apart into the mead ;
And to her bosom, with low-drooping lids,
Her face declined ; and down from her propp'd
    shoulders,
Her arms fell loosely ; and her slackening limbs,
Loosen'd out all her form ; and thus by him
She sloped ; in virgin ignorance unknowing
His fiery mood, or even the sympathy loosening
All her own make.   He gasp'd, his mouth did strive
'Neath suffocation ;—for beneath her eyes,
A dimly-flushing sultriness did increase,
And her lips out-sulk'd such a complaining sulk,
As though possess'd all conqueringly by desire,
And faintingly requiring love's moist balm.
He stood like one shot through with fixing pain ;
Recovering his purpose, with a cry,
He tore the talisman from his breast, and threw it

Towards her feet, and leapt into the wood.
Watching him swiftly stagger through the trees,
She reach'd the talisman ; it was a page
Scribed with his words, and kneeling she did read :
Her eyes seem'd straining down a vast abysm,
For some wing'd car to save ; her lips apart,
Her shoulders lifted, and her fingers clench'd,—
Show'd how she strove with hope, while read she
    there :—

"Oh ! beautiful girl, but one could love thee so !
When yestermorn sent thee stepping o'er the mead,
The thought of being adopt thine universe steed,
Doubled his life ;—thine universe steed, to go,
And against and through each fiercely-phalanx'd foe,
Bear thee all glorious ; in his heart bliss-fire,
That his broad frontage would itself attire,
With every wound aim'd towards thine overthrow :
And oh ! a thousand deaths seem'd less than nought,
Would'st thou but ride him through life's fiery storm ;
Burthening him fondly, thine affectionate form,
Whenever might peace be found or melody caught ;
When danger near'd, relinquishing proud all rein ;
When past, all fondly burthening him again.
But his will reins his heart ; and thereby rein'd

That heart is from the slightest start to love
Thee, who perchance its love might disapprove ;
For every love-plaint uninvitedly plain'd
Fouls ; yea, woman's purity is arraign'd,
When man thrusts towards her love-display, love-
　　claim,　　　　　·
She prompts not, cherishes not : what woman's
　　shame
But witnessing love she loves not, uncurtain'd ?
Then, beautiful girl ! though one could love thee so,
His passions in tumultuous armies, waiting
Worshippingly to convoy thee down time,
He wills not love ; exultingly shall go
His passions past thee, loudly jubilating
Towards life's fit ways, so crowdedly sublime."

The going radiance of the sinking sun
Was from the crimson sorrel yet undrawn,
When back return'd this chieftain of his passions,
King of his heart : as loitering, he came ;　　　·
Striving to twist his face into the forms
Of cold keen observation, such as make
With angular lines the countenances of those
Who scan phenomena. She still did kneel,
Her face bewilder'd white, and hued with pain.

One look she look'd to him,—its prompting feelings
Women perchance may know ; reproach was there,
Sadness was there,—yea, in its large fix'd eyes,
A questioning sadness that could make one's throat
Convulse with pity ; yet through all did rule
The deepest tenderness ;—

            " A lie ! a lie !
It was all lie !" he cried ; and at her feet
His face abased ; " your foot was on my neck ;
Had you withdrawn from me your trusting eyes,
Opening their avenues to some other gazer ;—
Oh God ! the imagining of the horror makes
The flesh to slide from my detested frame.—
I am calm ; my mind lifts up above my life,
I see it sovereignly ; this life of mine,
As it did tide beneath you, I will bare ;
Look you, and see how gloriously I lied.
I think,—but that through which I have been pass'd
Hath shaken the memory of earlier things :—
I think that ere we met life was to me,
As to most men, a whirl of beauteous mirage,
I still in vain pursued ; or sadly stood,
Mocking its hollowness ; the ponderous curse
Of unpursuit weighing deadeningly in my brain.
I know that when we met did all things change :
I nought pursued, yet passiveness was pleasure,

Being was bliss ; from all the outward things,
That make the total which mankind call life,
I was abstract ; or only then related,
When they did influence as subservient bonds
To bind us twain ;—the sunshine I did know,
Because that when its warmth relax'd my limbs,
I saw your arms fall also ; and the sea
I knew, because that when it awed my soul,
I saw your countenance gaze mysterious fear.
I had content ; my blood did pleasantly flow ;
Breathing was rest :—yet action that you urged
From the moment when my being prepared to act,
Till the moment that accomplished your will,
Was a delirious ecstasy,—the greater,
The greater the action that you did command.
And if 'twas bliss to be by you, and bliss
To act your will,—oh ! what the crushing torture,
To see another man look o'er your brow,
As he were fancying how divine his life,
Were it thus sway'd by yours ; to see another
Acquire your will, and with a happy smile,
Move for its service.   Other things now are come,
I know not whether to endure or curse.
Desire of you doth change my blood ; it burns ;
My veins start stiff, they tighten through my body,
They strangle me.   Oh girl ! what destiny is there,

That I am stricken thus ! I gaze against you ;
My baffled eyes see nought but murderous beauty ;
Your sound is beauty ; beauty are your robes ;
I dare not see your form beneath them move ;
And yet I see, and tremble, and die down.
" Oh, why is this ?" he moan'd through sobs, and roll'd
His body o'er the ground, " where is the peace,
The aforetime peace with which I blessingly loved you,
The rapture men call pure ?"

Two lips did press upon his fiery brow ;
They press'd, they stay'd, they lingeringly withdrew ;
He felt whole ages rolling o'er his life ;
Obliteratingly, ages roll'd away,
While those two lips his brow did apprehend
Gently to press themselves apart, and then
Gently to close again ; no word she said ;
Not otherwise she touch'd him ; he did never
Rise up his face to look ; but blindly wound
His arms around her sides, and to her bosom
Moved his still downcast head ; till there it dropt
In signless passiveness.
           Anon thèy rose,
Both pale as alabaster : summoning,
With a heavy sigh and compressure of her lips,

The needful force ;—her hand enclasp'd his arm,
Holding him opposite her, and with voice,
That came by syllables, distinct, she said,—
"I scarce know what men mean when name they love ;
I have not dream'd of life from you apart ;
Since many months I have not thought to hide
Aught that I feel from you ; it gave me joy,
When we have sympathized ; I never saw
Aught in you that offended me ; I would
Dare aught to make you happy or more good."

Thus all is over ; her concluding words
Were smother'd in his bosom ; for his arms
Had bound her to him, and her head had fall'n there.
The storm of feeling sank in both their beings
To the joy of rest ; upon the bank they sate ;
Over her shoulder lay his sinking face ;
Over his shoulder hers ; no words they spake,
No fast enlacements made they ; very softly,
And very timidly, close in her ear,
At last he whisper'd, " This is as I felt,
Those days I did lament, when peace was mine,
And love that men call pure ;" then gradually
Their faces they did lift ; and open-eyed,
They look'd unto each other, a look all free

From every questioning, or want, or aught
But love unutterable* :—'twas a look
Painter hath never limn'd, nor poet sung,
Nor dreamer vision'd, and could poet sound
Words that should give the minds of those who heard
Knowledge of its prompting feelings, he would fling
Art to the winds, thought, life, and heaven, forget,—
And though the uttering the words should shatter
Him to annihilation, he would speak,
And shatter himself into eternal fame.

* Nine lines here followed in the original edition which are
scored out in the two corrected copies, as "an untrue intrusion
into this place of the punishment that follows the gratification
of vile and degrading amours. Here (as all through the
volume) the immaturity and unsettled condition of the
author's ideas are very apparent."

THE RAILROAD.

WHY ! why to yon arch do the people drift,
Like a sea hurrying in to a cavern's rift,
Or like streams to a whirlpool streaming swift ?
     'Tis the railroad !
Each street and each causeway endeth there ;
And the whole of their peoples may step one stair
Down from the arch, and a power shall bear
Them swifter than wind from the mighty lair ;
     'Tis the railroad !

Pass through the arch ; put your ear to the ground !
This road sweepeth on through the isle and around !
You touch that which touches the country's bound !
     'Tis the railroad !
Like arrowy lightning snatch'd from the sky,
And bound to the earth, the bright rails lie ;

K

And their way is straight driven through mountains
    high.
And headland to headland o'er valleys they tie ;
                 'Tis the railroad !

See how the engine hums still on the rails,
While his long train of cars slowly down to him sails ;
He staggers like a brain blooded high, and he wails ;
                 'Tis the railroad !
His irons take the cars, and screaming he goes ;
Now may heaven warn before him all friends and all
    foes !
A whole city's missives within him repose,
Half a thousand miles his, ere the day's hours close ;
                 'Tis the railroad !

A PRAYER TO A FICKLE MISTRESS.

FROM the depth of my gloom to your beauty I come ;
But my gaze may not brighten, as erst, at its glow :
Nor kneel may I to you all gloriously low,
Nor feel your dear hand o'er my brow softly go ;
I know that you would that even now I sank dumb ;
    Lelia ! once say you are sad for me.

You would shrink, but to me, when mine eyes love
    did fight ;
When this arm clasp'd you round, 'midst your ravish-
    ing hair,
On this bosom loll'd your head, while unhidingly there
Your face turn'd to mine with such restful repair ;
God ! then how I dived in your eyes' surging light !
    Lelia ! once say you are sad for me.

Never God sent the night but I saw on my couch
Your cheek's beautiful sleep that I guarded supreme ;

Alone would I gaze till your soft lips would seem
There stirr'd by the mild light that round them did
    gleam ;—
Behind that chamber's madness horror-stricken I
    crouch !
        Lelia ! once say you are sad for me.

None could pity, I am hopeless ! I loved you to
    shame ;
Mine honour had been gone for one promising smile ;
When your soft hair fell cool o'er my burning face,
    while
My brain swoon'd with delight 'neath its curls ;—any
    guile
To be bless'd with thy bidding, had become my wild
    aim ;
        Lelia ! once say you are sad for me.

Your lover is coming ; I hear his wild vow !
For ever we are parting ; oh ! in mercy refrain
From that acted surprise ; I nor plead, nor complain ;
Oh ! yet say, when we loved, that thou didst not all
    feign,
And I'll bless thee, and pray for thee as to thee now ;
        Lelia ! once say you are sad for me.

A PAGAN'S DRINKING-CHAUNT.

LIKE the bright white arm of a young god, thrown
To the hem of a struggling maiden's gown,
The torrent leaps on the kegs of stone
That held this wine in the dark gulf down;
Deep five fathoms it lay in the cold,
The afternoon summer-heats heavily weigh;
This wine is awaiting in flagons of gold
On the side of the hill that looks over the bay.

There a bower of vines for each one bends
Under the terracing cedar-trees;
Where, shut from the presence of foes or friends,
He may quaff and couch in lonely ease;
The sunshine slants past the dark green cave,
In the sunshine the galleys before him will drowse;
And the roar of the town, like a far-travell'd wave,
Will faintly flow in to his calm carouse.

No restless womanhood frets the bower,
Exacting and fawning and vain and shy ;
But a beautiful boy shall attend the hour
And silently low in the entrance lie.
As he silently reads the scrolls that tell
The Cyprian's loves and the maiden's dreams,
His limbs will twine and his lips will swell,
And his eyes dilate with amorous schemes.

And his yearning limbs and his sultry mouth
Will recal to the drinker his own youth's prime ;
When there seem'd crowding round him from east,
    west, and south,
Countless sleek limbs of women with capturing mime ;
And he'll mourn for youth ; and he'll deem more dear
This cool bright wine ;—to our bowers, away !
And nothing will witness the sigh or the tear
On the side of the hill that looks over the bay.

DISMOUNTING A MISTRESS.

I TOUCH'D her lily hand !
  Earth, bound away !—
I' the stirrup did she stand ;
Her glorious foot I spann'd,
As she stepp'd to the land !—
  Where is the day ?

Where go ye, brother men ?
  Nought the same did stay !—
I went ; I turn'd agen ;
She kissed down the glen
Her fingers to me then !—
  Earth, bound away !

RAIN.

More than the wind, more than the snow,
More than the sunshine, I love rain;
Whether it droppeth soft and low,
Whether it rusheth amain.

Dark as the night it spreadeth its wings,
Slow and silently up on the hills;
Then sweeps o'er the vale, like a steed that springs
From the grasp of a thousand wills.

Swift sweeps under heaven the raven cloud's flight;
And the land and the lakes and the main
Lie belted beneath with steel-bright light,
The light of the swift-rushing rain.

On evenings of summer, when sunlight is low,
Soft the rain falls from opal-hued skies ;
And the flowers the most delicate summer can show
Are not stirr'd by its gentle surprise.

It falls on the pools, and no wrinkling it makes,
But touching melts in, like the smile
That sinks in the face of a dreamer, but breaks
Not the calm of his dream's happy wile.

The grass rises up as it falls on the meads,
The bird softlier sings in his bower,
And the circles of gnats circle on like wing'd seeds
Through the soft sunny lines of the shower.

THE FACE.

These dreary hours of hopeless gloom
Are all of life I fain would know;
I would but feel my life consume,
While bring they back mine ancient woe;
For midst the clouds of grief and shame
They crowd around, one face I see;
It is the face I dare not name;
The face none ever name to me.

I saw it first when in the dance
Borne, like a falcon, down the hall,
He stay'd to cure some rude mischance
My girlish deeds had caused to fall;
He smiled, he danced with me, he made
A thousand ways to soothe my pain;
And sleeplessly all night I pray'd
That I might see that smile again.

I saw it next, a thousand times;
And every time its kind smile near'd;

Oh ! twice ten thousand glorious chimes
My heart rang out, when he appear'd ;
What was I then, that others' thought
Could alter so my thought of him !
That I could be by others taught
His image from my heart to dim !

I saw it last, when black and white,
Shadows went struggling o'er it wild ;
When he regain'd my long-lost sight,
And I with cold obeisance smiled ;—
I did not see it fade from life ;
My letters o'er his heart they found ;
They told me in death's last hard strife
His dying hands around them wound.

Although my scorn that face did maim,
Even when its love would not depart,
Although my laughter smote its shame,
And drave it swording through his heart,
Although its death-gloom grasps my brain
With crushing unrefused despair ;—
That I may dream that face again
God still must find alone my prayer.

WHIMPER OF AWAKENING PASSION.

Your hands made a tent o'er mine eyes,
As low in your lap I was lain,
Perhaps half from yourself to disguise
The prayer that they could not restrain.*

You sang, and your voice through me waved
Such rapture, I heard myself say,
"Oh here is the heaven I have craved,
Never hence will I wander astray."

As I lay in your lap your limbs gave
Such beautiful smooth rest to me,
I told you that thus to be slave
I would never consent to be free.

* The opening stanza runs thus in the original edition :—

Your hands were a tent for mine eyes,
As low in your lap I was lain ;
And I thought as I gazed at my skies,
I will never know other again.

But now mine eyes under their tent
Think such distance from yours, love, is wrong;
And my mouth wants your mouth to be sent
Down to him, all undrest, love, of song.

Oh I fear if your beautiful limbs
Still to have me their slave feel inclined,
You must either prevent all these whims,
Or a way, love, to humour them find.

A LADY'S HAND.

It is the same bright fairy dress
That robes thy beauteous form,
And with the same unstartled grace
Thou gazest o'er the storm ;
The same mysterious hour
Now girdles round us twain ;
Lay then, in this same bower,
Thy hand on me again.

Thy hand on me again, lady !
All man's world sleepeth still ;
And God hath given the rein, lady,
To his world's passionate will.
See how the lightnings leap, lady,
Over the rocks and the main ;
Oh ! lay, while all men sleep, lady,
Thy hand on me again.

The storm around us rife
Befits the storm that then
Will rise amidst my life,
With the same wild joy as when
At this same midnight hour,
When thus raged heaven and main,
In this same secret bower,
Thy hand did not refrain.

On me again that hand, lady,
Nearer the thunder peals ;
The chains on my heart disband, lady,
Now, now, while Nature reels,
While sleeps all life like the grave, lady,
But ours and the hurricane,—
While now thou may'st yet save, lady,
Thy hand on me again !

THE POET'S DEATH.

Now the Poet's death was certain, and the leech had
    left the room ;
Only those who fondly loved him waited to receive
    the doom ;
And the sister he loved best, whiter than hemlock did
    veer ;
And she bent, and " Life is going" faintly whisper'd in
    his ear.

Though her fingers clasp'd his fingers, though her
    cheek by his did lay,
Though she whisper'd "I am dying ; with thee, death
    hath no dismay ;"
Fiercely sprang the startled Poet, and his eye did
    fight through space,
While dark agony did thicken his drawn lips and
    wrench his face.

Sister arms did wind around him, knelt his sire beside
    the bed ;
And his mother busied round him, love extinguishing
    her dread ;
But the Poet heeded nothing, fixing still his fighting
    eye,
Gathering, gathering, gathering inward that he was
    that hour to die.

Now the sound of smother'd sobbings smote upon his
    distant mind,
And he turn'd a glance around him, that each gazer's
    love divined ;
The torture in his face did stagger once before his
    mother's look ;
Then came back more whiteningly, while his neck did
    downward crook.

From his crook'd-down neck, his visage struggled
    love back through its pain,
First to one, and then to another, and then left them
    all again ;
As the sister wept against him, shudderingly to her
    he turn'd ;
And his lips did open at her, and his eyes for language
    yearn'd.

Quick at her his lips did open, strivingly his eyelids
    rose,
But no sound, no word, no murmur, their fast ges-
    turings did disclose;
Straightly pointed he his arm then where his poet-
    desk was lain;
To his grasp the sister brought it, while the stillness
    throbb'd amain.

From his desk the Poet tore the unform'd scriptures
    of his soul;
And to them he fiercely pointed, while his eyes large
    tears did roll;
"Perfected, my memory earth to endless time would
    love and bless;
I must die, and these will live not!" through his lips
    at last did press.

Whiter grew the gazing faces, as the cliffs that sun-
    shine smites,
When they found no aid could come from earthly
    loves, or priestly rites;
O'er his scriptures he fell forward, and they all did
    trust and say
That the last wild pang was on him, for as still as
    stone he lay.

But than lightning's flash more sudden, he did spurn
    the abhorred bed ;
And a moment he stood tottering, toss'd defyingly
    his head ;
Ere one reach'd him, he was fallen, lifeless, and his
    wide dull'd eye
Rigid with the fierce defiance that had just refused to
    die.

To the gloomy troop of Atheists gibberingly the
    sister ran,
While the praying father kneeling hurl'd at her his
    pious ban ;
In the churchyard lies the Poet, and his smell the air
    depraves ;
And ten thousand thousand like him stuff the earth
    with such-like graves.

A COMING CRY.

THE few to whom the law hath given the earth God
    gives to all
Do tell us that for them alone its fruits increase and
    fall ;
They tell us that by labour we may earn our daily
    bread,
But they take the labour for their engines that work
    on unfed ;
And so we starve ; and now the few have publish'd
    a decree,—
Starve on, or eat in workhouses the crumbs of
    charity ;
Perhaps it's better than starvation,—once we'll pray,
    and then
We'll all go building workhouses, million, million
    men !

We'll all go building workhouses,—million, million
    hands,
So jointed wondrously by God, to work love's wise
    commands ;
We'll all go building workhouses,—million, million
    minds,
By great God charter'd to condemn whatever harms
    or binds ;
The God-given mind shall image, the God-given hand
    shall build
The prisons for God's children by the earth-lords will'd;
Perhaps it 's better than starvation, once we'll pray,
    and then
We'll all go building workhouses,—million, million
    men.

What 'll we do with the workhouses ? million, million
    men !
Shall we all lie down, and madden, each in his lonely
    den ?
What ! we whose sires made Cressy ! we, men of
    Nelson's mould !
We, of the Russells' country,—God's Englishmen the
    bold !

Will we, at earth's lords' bidding, build ourselves dis-
　　honour'd graves ?

Will we who've made this England, endure to be its
　　slaves ?

Thrones totter before the answer !—once we'll pray,
　　and then

We'll all go building workhouses,—million, million
　　men.

A PLEA FOR LOVE OF THE INDIVIDUAL.

It were to live not! Lady, cease thy pleading,
"Love not, love not," — words indeed "vainly ·
    spoken;"
The heart will love even when torn and bleeding,
Yea, love that very one by whom 'tis broken :
           Oh love then ! love !

Love ! love ! though it be true the loved may change;
For thine agony in his alien caressing
Will sink to a sad calm, and cannot estrange
Thy power to love him still with measureless blessing :
           Oh love then ! love !

Yea, even then loving, when pales with fear his brow
At his own inconstancy,—thou shalt awaken
To a wild sweet bliss in striving more to endow
With beauty and truth the one for whom thou wert
    forsaken :
           Oh love then ! love !

Love ! love ! albeit the loved may die,—yet love !
Canst not thou die ? the loving grave-descender
Burns with a rapturous joy that never may move
The unloving wanderer down whole lives of splendour:
   Oh love then ! love !

Though one brief love-hour order years of sorrow,
Love ! love ! for that one hour will make thee know
How, long as earth rolls round from morn to morrow,
Will its myriad peoples pant with love's wild glow :
   Oh love then ! love !

Yea ! for this knowledge even from oblivion's tomb
Banishes disgust ; who, who disdains to end,
Knowing the love-bliss that while life shall bloom,
Over his grave shall deepeningly expend ?
   O love then ! love !

PLEA FOR LOVE OF THE UNIVERSAL.

NAY, minstrel, love ! and all things round thee
    moving
Shall utter heavenly music, smile thee light ;
For mighty is the loveliness of loving
    To endue the loved with joy, and joy makes bright ;.
        Oh love then ! love !

Love magnifies existence ; love the world,—
    Thy soul shall grow world-great in its sensation ;
And 'neath the blaze of infinite life unfurl'd,
    Pant with the passion of a whole creation.
        Oh love then ! love !

For thine own heart's sake, love ! the unloving mind,.
    Unemanating light, no light receiveth ;
Tomb of itself, unable rest to find,
    Buried alive, it low and wildly grieveth.
        O love then ! love !

Why sayest thou " Love not, for the loved may die !"
   Reasoning inadequate !—because trees wither,
Do suns cease shining ? though one loved thing fly,
   Sends it not others love-desiring hither ?
            Oh love then ! love !

And thy warning "Love not, for the loved may
      change,"
   Discrediteth love, that never a fee requires ;
Happy in loving, though all, all be strange,
   Its flame still burns, itself feeds still its fires :
            Oh love then ! love !

Love is that act which maketh rich in giving ;
   Passion of soul which wasteth not, nor paineth ;
Battled for, pray'd for, wept for, by all living ;
   Dwelling most in him who most of happiness
      gaineth :
            Oh love then! love !

WAYS OF REGARD.

SHARKS' jaws are glittering through the eternal ocean
Now, even as ever; through its topmost seas
That mightily billow, through the secrecy
Of its abysms, where the waters bide
Omnipotently shuddering,—scattering fear,
Onward they go; their illuminating teeth
Perpetually parting; and ever through
Some dolphin's body nervously they clench.
Hidden within the tropic forest's maze,
Now, even as ever, glares the tiger's eye
Over its victim, yellow-circling light:
And there the serpent, with his gaze, still charms
To approach, and into his distended jaws
Shiveringly hie the gaudy chattering parrot,
Or gambolling coney: and shaggy spiders there
Catch in their webs the flitting humming-birds:

And through the golden air, the humming-birds flitting
Slay countless happy insects.

                             Slaughter sways
Supremely everywhere : where man comes not,
Beasts kill each other; where his empire holds,
There, oh ye gods ! on richer aliment
Feeds slaughter, and extends.   There armies clash ;
And in the shock ten thousand human forms,
Each with all exquisite joints and countless nerves,
Fall bloodily broken.   There the priest-piled faggots
Flame round the martyr, and send up to heaven
The smoke of torment.   There the blood-stain'd hands
Of gold-holders sell sustenance to the goldless,
At price of body, at price of mind and heart.
There the goldless pay this price, and breed successors;
A generation of things that never live,
But toil, and suffer, and shriek,—undead abortions,
That yet are human children !   And self-slain,
Often humanity.   Man's towns and cities
Seem builded on rivers, that the rushing waters
May roll for him the ever-ready tomb
He oft assumes ; and self-slain, ever go down
Fond women, who the cup of life still spill,
Offering it tremblingly to some gallant's lips.

Dire is the woe, when first the vision of slaughter,
Thus everywhere regnant, breaks into the mind,
Youthful and loving, and emerging from the home
Where all it knew was that all round it smiled ;
And whence ever went its fancies, towards some fate
That should one day lead it through the maze of life,
To seek and share love everywhere.   At first,
Stunn'd like a wader out into the sea,
Who thinking he steps upon the sand, finds only
Water yield under him,—the appalled youth,
Withouten speech or thought, instinctively,
Reaches out aimlessly and in vain for aid.
Then the howl of the world arouses him ; he rises,—
Through heavens and hells, eternities and times,
Wildly he stares ;—seeking the power that bids
This terrible reign.   Baffled, his gaze retreats ;
He strips his being of all control and veil,
With which men gird themselves ; and he thinks his
        teeth
Could grasp Earth's wretched breast, and that he
        could leap
With her to oblivion.   And while thus he dreams,
Steals sensual pleasure to him.   The nakedness
To which in his noble rage he smote his being
But exposes him to her dalliance ; and he turns
From thought that bids him hurl against the unknown

His life, that itself dishonours in enduring
Sight of the blood-stain'd universe,—to the arms
Of sensual pleasure, and exhausted there,
Finds ignominious sleep ;—
If sleep that be, whereunto ever descend
The visions of possible and gentle glory,
That circled brightly round his youth, and that now
Invite him, from his impotent degradation,
To soar unto their joy ;—if sleep that be,
From which the sleeper must ever rise, and slay,
With a murder worse than parricide, these entreaters;—
Or awake, to find his moral powers gone idiot,
And his intellect sane to watch them.

    But many there are who know the scheme of life,
A plan for battle and murder, yet undergo
Nor fear, nor rage.   With energy they strain
Life's murderous principle to their use to curb.
Earth, bleeding, drags her chain ; but a car thereto
These ones do fasten ; and therein they sit,
In *their* happiness, and *their* pride, all sumptuously.
Also are those, whose minds will never take
A world-wide vision ; and who mete life's merits
By their own present circumstance.   When shines,
Full on their skins, the sun,—this life they call

A beautiful home ; and when they suffer one
Of the world's evils,—maundering for death,
The self-same life they cry a torture-house.
These pester, with charge of morbidness and disease,
Those of their brethren, in whose world-wide hearts,
Earth's misery ever sticks, a poisoning knife.
And beings unhuman are there who regard
This universal slaughter never as man.

The general mind knows only things that impinge
Its palpable senses ;—otherwise, haughty steps
Of men who tread with appropriating feet
Earth and its causeways ; and of beauteous women,
Who walk our pavements and our terraces,
And our swung bridges, as though hoveringly
Their scornful feet the fitness questioned
Of every spot they press,—would drop to the shuffle
Of slaves and tools.   Yea ! had man the vision
That sees all being, he would scramble on
Athwart his fields, and his hills, and through all his
        streets,
With the abased hurry of one, who moves
A petty unit in a round of motion,
By other intelligences curiously scann'd,
And for their study begotten.   Yea! would he

Pause in his being, and question whether to end.
He would check the lion-like passions, which him
    prompt
To complete the sovereignty of slaughter; and ask
Whether, like wild beasts for the Roman's sport,
His groups should tear themselves, that unhuman
    powers
May study the unity which through creation
Most orderly dwells.

        One saw, commanding time,
And extinguishing space, and past the farthest reach
Of the five senses reaching,—he beheld,
Within this earth, when night was dark, a cavern,
Peopled with slaves contemplating revolt.
Under the light of many a lurid fire
That burn'd on upper ledges of the rock,
The countless slaves stood noiselessly; the light
Fell on the mass, as eagerly it upheld
Its faces to the chief, who on a ledge
Above them stood. In tumult lifted it
Its wither'd countenances, skinny jaws,
Wild eyes, and knotted brows, and bloodless lips.
One after the other rose the faces, till
They settled there, one pale dark stare of pain.

Passing the crowded slaves, towards the chief,
There rush'd a woman ; with the gasping utterance
Of fear, she shriek'd unto the chief, " Your daughter !
Your daughter has been ravish'd ! In the grove,
She rush'd by where I stood, and after her
The lord, your master. Furiously obscene
Were his wild oaths. I follow'd him ; I saw
Him snatch her from the precipice she had climb'd ;
He took her in his arms ; he laid him down
Beside her senseless form ; I knelt to him ;
And by his mother's fame, his sister's honour,
By his own manhood, by her helplessness,
Pray'd him for pity on her chastity.
He spat in her face, and laugh'd ; I snatch'd his
    knife,
And should have slain him ; but he wrested it,
Pinion'd my arms, and to the nearest tree
Bound me. Her screaming shudder'd on my cheek :
The wind swept, but it waved no death-sword !
The stars shone, but afar, and placidly !
Clouds hurried through the air, but no avenger
Burst from their gloom ! the hill, the poison'd hill,
Stirr'd not ! I heard his oaths, his laughs, his blows,
Sound out in the clear night. I could not stir ;
My impotence was crime ; one terrible shriek
Struck my heart void. Oh ! nothing more I know."

M

The mechanism of the chieftain's frame
Shook for a moment while this tale began;
Then evidenced not emotion, save by pallor
That through his frame did deepen,—the same pallor
As that within the murder'd victim's face,
At the last blow of many.   When the silence
Throbb'd through the cavern, he arose, and cried,
" Why tell you that your sister and my child,
Struck from the pedestal of maidenhood
To the cold ditch of harlotry, outcrieth
Her pain, her terror; that the coming hours
Still bring the fiend who dash'd her; that unhinder'd
He aye repeats his brutal ravishment !
That presently, tired of his victim, he,
From utter hatred of her chaster nature,
Will thrust her o'er to indiscriminate rape;
Make her sweet form the sink of filthiness;
Yea, for the merriment of his gazing comrades,
Force her to crimes unnatural, too monstrous
For words to image ! I insult the maiden,
Proclaiming thus her wrongs, for you abet them !
She shrieks to us for aid; your lying eyes
Smile to her ravisher !—Do thou, God ! hear me !
Hear, God ! Not even my child herself supposeth
The blackness low impending o'er her life.
She will not keep her virtues : she must change ;

The filth perpetually assailing her
Must alter her ! 'Tis not in human nature,
Endless repulsion.   O that she could know—
For then her life would shudder out at once—
Know that the very horrors she now hates
She shall lust after ;—that her soul shall suit
Its nature to its circumstance, until
Its wings shall rotten off, its plumage drop,—
Till it become a naked leprous remnant
To whom death dares not open paradise.
Hear, God ! this daughter of thine own shall start,
And fight against herself, and doubt her being ;
She shall begin to fear that she may change ;
She shall think that she may change ; her thought
    will grow
Into belief ;—then ever, ever, ever,
The spectre of her future self shall haunt her ;
She dares not hate it, yet she must, she does ;
Like to a serpent-fascinated bird,
She loathes yet runs to it.
Oh ! worse than every other agony,
Thou keenest consciousness of vilest crime,
—This struggling amidst darkness of the soul ;
—This giving o'er the struggle when all palsied
She first perceives that irredeemably
She is changing to the foulness she abhors :

Her wild doom, like a vast upstanding sea,
Unnatural, overhangs!

              Slaves! brothers! are we
Already thus cursed? Damn'd are we to endurance,
To acquiescence, to contentment? Oh! not so!
The habit of obedience hath not slain ye!
Arise! shake out the fetters from your souls,
And they will leave your limbs! All is not lost.
Hear me, oh hear me! We no more are slaves;—
Have we not hearts like men? do we not feel
The voice of kindness, contemplate with pleasure
The joys of life? are not our senses human?
Own we no love; can we not love return?
Oh! being men, they who would hold you slaves,
Do murder you alive! They blind your minds
With writhing toil, and say you have no sight;
They break you from the majesty of man
Into gaunt monsters, crooked miseries,
And call you brute-like,—trample down your hearts,
And say you have none,—banish from your souls
The light of knowledge, and proclaim you soulless,—
Rend you from God, saying you are not men :—
But that we are, witness this hungering dagger
Which through his troops of hireling cut-throats,

And through his massive towers, and through his
    silks,
Shall reach my daughter's ravisher's heart, and stab
Right through its damned core, there thundering,
The *man*, your slave ! Aha ! have you no daughters ?
Where are your wives ? your sweethearts ? Spitten
    upon !
Beaten in the face while ravish'd ! Ha ! you start !
Prove, prove that you are men ! Revenge ! re-
    venge !—
They bade us feed on grass—we will grow drunk
With their red blood ; they trample us as snakes—
We will rise dragon-like, and with our fetters
Act inconceivably !—Revenge ! revenge !
Not that they violate our wives for sport,
And laugh at our unnatural endurance,—
Not that they tear our children from their mothers,
Crippling their limbs, extinguishing their minds
With endless toil,—the only things that love us,—
Not that our food is garbage ; that our babes
Droop at the milkless teat ;—not that they dare,
Oh shameless beasts ! unnaturally deprive
Our youth of manhood,—
But because that they have so damned us
That we've endured these shames ! Oh for *this*
    murder,

This poisoning, this pollution, this dead life,
What, what revenge ! They lash us into smiles !
God ! we will rush through blood up to our arm-
    pits ! "—
He ceased, o'ercome with passion ; his clench'd
    hands
Signing the fury that had choked his voice,
And roll'd his eyeballs backward. In the cave
Each auditor foams fiercely with his mouth ;
Motionless where he stood, and listen'd, and shook.
With horrible imprecations at their lords,
With wordless yells, they rage around the cave
Like madden'd tigers ; tearing each other's flesh
And pledging murder with the outspurting gore.
Amidst the uproar gasps the chief ; his hair
Cresting ; his hands clutch'd up in vacancy ;
And an inward light burns lurid in his face,
Like the reflection of a burning kingdom ;
And backward from his gnashing teeth are drawn
And fix'd his lips.

        One saw, commanding time
And extinguishing space, and past the farthest reach
Of the five senses reaching,—he beheld
Glide from this cavern, while thus the chieftain ceased,

A young man and a maiden.   To that caste,
Whereat the chief did rage, did both belong
By birth and circumstance ; yet the young man,
By sympathy for the oppress'd, to the slaves
Felt himself bound.   And she, the maiden with him,
Loved him ; and therefore thought his feelings
    noblest,
And therefore shared them.   On his shoulder leans
    she
One hand ; and opposite to him she stands.
Her pity-parted lips and glistening eyes
Answer the chief's harangue, and anxiously ask
Her lover's interference.   Yet she waits,
All confident that he will end this shame ;
That now he will tell her how.   Yea ! never,
Shall Christian, opening out his household bible
When hours of anguish crowd round threateningly—
Never shall soldier, while around his sword's hilt
Putting a quiet hand, when tramp of foemen
Catches his ear—shall pole-star seeing sailor—
God, self-contemplating—feel confidence
More perfectly assured than that which beam'd
Light through this maiden's quivering tears, when
    lines
Of high resolve, made architectural
The face of her love ; of him, her sword, her bible,

Her guiding star, her God omnipotent.—
For woman, in the idolatry of her love,
Believeth him in whom her soul reposes
Ever as divine in power as in will.
And then the young man answers—partly himself,
And partly her, and partly unpresent things,
Addressing passionate :—" And what were I
But a superior, a more criminal slave,
Should I retreat to my abodes and pleasures,
Leaving these wretched ones uncounsell'd thus ?
Give a man all his rights, and these alone,
He's a high animal, a noble brute !
Crown him with duty, and you make him man ;
King of himself, and equal citizen
Of all earth's populaces.   Glorious duty !
Give me thy crown, and though its weight be death,—
Dying, I'll crown myself.   Yea, plunder'd slave !
Yet shalt thou know what glorious exultation,
The consciousness of liberty ; a joy
Vast as the courser's, when in lonely freedom
He rushes wave-like o'er the gusty hill-top,
Kicking his heels into the rivalling wind.
And thou shalt know too what divine repose
Accomplish'd duty yields.   Thou hast no self :
Oh monstrous contradiction !—thou, possessing
A cursed identity, yet having no power

To self-determinate,—a tortured tool
For others' usage, which, when overworn,
Is flung aside to rot. You might have homes,
And gambolling children, and affectionate wives;
You might be loving, wise; for you are men!
Man is eternal; tyrants and slavery
Are but the tricks of time.   Within the senate,
I'll taunt our nobles, till they drag their crowns
Down on their brows to hide the blush of shame.
If I move not the king to piteous thought,
His lip shall whiten.   All their boasted order,
Their laws unbroken, all the deep submission
Of their whipp'd slaves,—is terrible disorder;
Disorder of the universe and of the heart.
They shall know anarchy is abroad, more dread
That her wild step is noiseless, that her form
Is undistinguishable, save at times
By the red fires that in the yards of law
Curl round rebellious serfs; while then her bearing
Hath not the noble fierceness of a storm-god,
But with assassin calmness her cold smile
Measures a secret dagger.   They outcry,
" The nation flourishes, its power is vast,"
" Its wealth supreme."   Oh idiot knaves and liars!
Say, is a flag a nation? is an army?
Do half a million traders make a nation?

A thousand lords ?   The people is the nation ;
If they be slaves, if they be suffering,
The power, the majesty, the wealth you boast,
Is tinsel hiding the rottenness you ordain !
And much they prate of station.   Much they say
Touching God-order'd ranks.   Me they accuse
Of rendering slaves superior to that state,
In which, they say, it has pleased God to place them !
They counsel—if your slave seem fond of freedom,
Starve him, till he be glad to lick your foot
And then get crumbs ; if he would fain be wise,
Work him, until the writhing of his body
Shall suffocate his mind ; if he would love,
And husband womanhood, let famish'd children
Of others terrify ; even from his birth
Palsy his heart with fear, darken his soul,
Defile his body.   Yea ! this mutilation
They do advise, when smilingly they say,
Be slaves so educate, that to their stations,
Their natures may be fitted.   " Educate ! "
Ye villains sacrilegious, who would rob
God's human temple of its majesty,
That ye may stable there in barbarous pomp !
Misname not thus your murderous reduction
Of beauty into baseness, man to brute.
Man has no station ; he must upward soar

Towards bright-wing'd deities, or sink down towards
 fiends ;
Man cannot pause.—
Go ! bid the sun to rot within its heavens !
Arrest the marching melodies of stars !
Chill every river into stagnancy !
Deracinate the fruitful earth of growth !
Though infinite space grow dark, the soul of man
Shall soar triumphantly.   Within this cavern
Are thousands, sworn to rise from out the mire,
Whereto you damn them ; they will rise,—will rise,
Though war may hew their pathway, though their
 march
Be in blood to the armpits !   Oh that it were mine
To lead them bloodless conquerors !   They will rise,—
But with the chains they shatter from their limbs,
Must they do hellishly.   A vessel, laden
With captives fetter'd unto famine and plague,
Now is this land ; the slaves force-freed, will make it
A burning wreck ; themselves amidst the flames,
Maniacs, wild dancing.   Oh who, who can know,
How to redeem this people ? "

       All this heard
The seer ; and more than this harangue did proffer

Unto the ear, the seer beheld, and took,
Down in the young man's countenance.   And now
Came from the cave a statesman ; his high brow
All restless with anxiety ; to himself
He mutter'd as he walk'd,—" The fools I serve
Under pretence of ruling, to whose whims
Aye must I pander, and the pandering call
Government ; for whose robbery of their fellows
That have no gold, I ever forge skilful tools
And term them law—will sooner or later rue
The existence of this slavery.   A power
Repress'd, yet gathering, and without a vent
For its intenseness, must in every body
Do certain death.   A power must either serve
For or against the thing in which it dwells ;
Neutral it cannot be."   And on he shuffled,
For there were none to watch him grandly walk ;
And as he went, continued he, " These fools
Would hurl me from my eminence and renown,
Told I them truth ; why should I lose my power,
To gain their hatred ?   The uncouth revolters
A little while can be repress'd, and so
Repress'd shall be ; while I acquire the fame
Of wise, bold statesmanship."   With a dark sneer
At human error ; and chuckling out these words—
" Let the future look to it,"—the statesman pass'd.

Him follow'd one, not lofty in the state,
Not low, but finding there the middle rank ;
The rank which 'twixt the lowest and the highest
Lifts an impassable barrier, and like
A voluntary lackey, ever kicks
The lowest lower.   Rank, whose envy is
To have some other under it ; whose hope
Is to merge into the highest ; and whose action
Is getting gold to administer these desires.
His white lip writhed, as from the cave he rush'd
In savage wrath.   " Our constitution, order,
Obedience, command are jeoparded ;
No slaves ! no master ! Even upon ourselves,
The beasts would have us tend ! By all that is
Holy and reverend ; by our household hearths,
These fiends would desecrate ; by the constitution,
Our fathers have bequeathed us ; if there be
Virtue in law and armies,—a swift cure
Shall find these wretched levellers ; "—this creature,
Able to reason on the modes of serving
His purposes and his instincts, but no more ;
Forgetting, or unable to examine
Those instincts or those wills ;—cried, rushing on
Towards his home, the thought within him burning
That his dear children's sumptuousness and grace
Were based upon this slavery.

The seer saw on :
And the cavern still shook with uproar, and the fury
Therein wax'd devilish.   Swiftly from its mouth,
Swifter than a river hurl'd from off a star
That rolls uncheck'd, stream'd high to the empyrean
Radiance of powers unhuman.   In a moment,
Above all lower firmaments, and above
All clouds and winds, it soar'd.   Immortal calm
Received its glory.   To the immortal calm
The unhuman powers rush'd,—as rushes one
From drinking in some exquisite music tones,
To shun all else, and in unpeopled space
Breathe rapturously.   They circled round and round ;
Now sweeping vast and rapture-uttering curves,
Now floating tremulously with happiness,
Now solemnly moving in elated thought
Of their own grandeur ; while in unison,
Circled above the seer their measured song.
"The baptism of the earth speeds swiftly on !
Earth's human things pour bounteously their blood !
Rejoice, companions !   Soon will be complete
Auxiliar changes, and one mighty change
Glorious outburst.   No doubt disturbs our joy ;
Assured of the universe's truth,
We wait expectant.   To her sister worlds
Soon shall we convoy this long-travail'd planet ;

Our pleasures thrill'd to that ecstatic bliss,
With which we watch'd the sun mount up in chaos,
Before him wildernesses of shade dissolving,
Till where he paused, towards him swiftly sail'd
The numberless stars that worshipping round him
    move.
Rejoice, companions ! All earth's crowded creatures
Leaven it for its fate, unfalteringly.
And the blood and passion which must yet be spill'd
Into its substance, with a tenfold richness
Sink o'er it now. The creatures of its youth
Were few and passionless, and they spill'd them-
    selves
Half niggardly. But now quick human things
Throng gloriously redundant; and they spring
In armies to their calling; and they fall,
Of measureless passion full.—Herein is love !
The movements of all things still gradual quicken,
That followingly may our contemplation large
From happiness to ecstasy. Rejoice !
Rejoice, companions ! on this embryo star,
As on a myriad earlier ones, men grow
Thick as the nebulæ of the galaxy ;
As on a myriad other ones, they pour
Oceans of blood and passion into her veins ;
That, as a myriad other ones, this star

May shudder into a thousand different moods,—
The happiness of her changings never the same,
Ever increased and different.   Even now
The race of man is culminating !   Now,
Big is the earth with the superior creatures
Waiting to displace man.   Their glorious slaughters,
Their frenzied passions, their quick-ended lives,
Await our gaze.   Oh, sweep, sweep on, companions,
And glory in our delight !   We still remain ;
All undisturb'd our high prerogative   .
Of blissful contemplation.   Though we know
Nought of the emotions which the short-lived children
Of earth, and all the planets, impart and share,—
Be ye sure that even when their faces whiten,
And their forms rend each other, and the air
Rocks with their outcry,—not even then, nor ever,
Reach they our bliss contemplative.   We remain !
All things beneath us change, and still we take
From every change fresh joy.   Beneath us roll
Differently all things ; everything us yields
Joy differently.   Sweep, sweep on, companions !
And glory in our delight.   Eternally
All things intensify ; and we must ever
Intenselier contemplate, intenselier joy.
Rest we above the cave.   Rejoice, companions !
Brightly speeds on the baptism of the earth."

FEMININE SPITE.

THE trial was over; for stolen gold,
Robin the gardener his life had sold;
The judge had commended to heaven his soul,
And his head from the guillotine's hatchet to roll;
The maiden who loved him did speed to his cell,
And her brain shook with fear, like a vibrating bell,
When there purposely met her the black-hair'd
    Lucette,
Whose grass-flipping feet show'd the village coquette.

This black-hair'd Lucette oft had striven to make
A suitor of Robin;—at church, and at wake,
With her eyes in the dance, with her leg at the stile,
With her romps in the fields, she had striven to
    beguile
The senses of Robin, that so he might pray
Her mercy, and she, with disdain, answer nay;
But no looking, no romping, no unveiling would do,
To the maiden who loved him poor Robin was true.

N

Now to meet this lorn maiden, Lucette had put on
Her flauntiest of dresses, her blackest shoes shone
Against her white stockings, her white and red
    gown
Was tassell'd with ribands, around, up and down ;
She saw the maid sobbing,—her bright greedy eye
Just glanced all around to see no one was nigh,—
Then she sniff'd, and she smirk'd, and she toss'd back
    her head,
And " You're lucky to know the young gardener," she
    said.

FEMININE GOODNESS.

Soft to her bower the letter came,
  Where dreaming bliss she sigh'd;
And signed by her lover's name
  It claims her for his bride;
Like cloudless skies of summer night
  One hour before the day,
Where in the east translucent light
  Beneath the dark doth play,—
Her eyes well up with beauteous sheen,
  For though she knew 't would come,
'Tis fresh excess of happiness,
  To clasp it thus-wise home.

But ere she left the bower, there fill'd
  Another light those eyes;

Two crystal tear-drops o'er them thrill'd,
   And half disguised their skies ;
But holier far than tears of joy,
   Than tears of maiden fear,
They started for some gentle boy
   Who'd found their glance too dear.
And, oh ! were I her lover, I
   Had rather found her now,
Than when her eyes shone bright replies
   To my recorded vow.

"Car la pensée a aussi ses ivresses, ses extases, ses voluptés célestes, dont une heure vaut toute une jeunesse, toute une vie."— GEORGE SAND.

Of all the suns that over earth have smiled,
The summer's evening sun I love the best;
Because it ray'd when I beheld a child
Come from the cedar grove, at home to rest.

His wide-orb'd eyelids moved not as he came;
His cheeks were pale; his eyes were heavily bright;
His lips were parted movelessly; pale flame
Around his mouth play'd quietly pale delight.

His forest dog went bounding to his side;
His eyes veer'd slowly towards the fawning hound,
But kept their fixedness, pre-occupied
With thought, whence other thoughts did all rebound.

His beautiful mother took his drooping hand;
And when he lavish'd on her no caress,

—" What ails my boy ? " from across her soul's large
    land,
Pass'd through her lips, with ravishing gentleness.

" Mother, I know not ; to the cedar trees
I chased a butterfly ; it danced too high,
And left me underneath ; the evening breeze
Came with me there, and there it seem'd to die.

" And all was silent as the minster's nave
On common days ; upon the ground I sate,
And reverence closed mine eyes, as with the wave
 Of silent and of soundless passing state.

" Anon mine eyelids lifted, and I saw
Above me terracing the mighty trees ;
The sun continuing utterly to withdraw
His rays from out them, by composed degrees.

" When the rays all were taken, and unlit
The grove gloom'd dark, again mine eyes did close,
And in my mind, where lonely I did sit,
The memory of the high priest's blessing rose.

" As from the scene towards this thought I gazed,
A mighty ecstasy through my brain did go,
Like overwhelming ocean ; cresting, raised
My hair, while I did cower and tremble low ;

" For both one essence possess'd ;—the cedar-grove,
Spreading its shadowing bows high o'er me there ;
And the priest's hands outstretch'd my head above,
Solemnly sheltering me, with voiceless prayer.

" It seem'd as though into my brain did roll
A thunder-cloud, that burst in bright wild rain,
Torrenting through my limbs, and for its goal,
Mounting back mightily to my brain again.

" I am not sad, mother ; I have no ill,
But a great storm within me doth subside ;
The ebbing of rapture wearies me ; still, still,
Me alone leave, dear mother ;" the boy replied.

Ceasing, he kissed her with serious pride,
The while his hand carress'd the hound's large head ;
And then away he seriously did glide,
And I retired where'er my footsteps led.

Deems any this vision insufficient cause
That I should love the hour that gave it me,
Oh ! knew he his own human-nature's laws,
Much would he yearn to have been given it to see.

The essence of mind's being is the stream of thought;
Difference of mind's being is difference of the stream;
Within this single difference may be brought
The countless differences that are or seem.

Now thoughts associate in the common mind
By outside semblance, or from general wont ;
But in the mind of genius, swift as wind,
All similarly influencing thoughts confront.

Though the things thought, in time and space, may lie
Wider than India from the Arctic zone ;
If they impress one feeling, swift they fly,
And in the mind of genius take one throne.

This order of mind is shaken to the core
With mighty joy, while therewithin cohere
Its far-brought thoughts; o'er the common mind's dull
    floor,
As of old, its thoughts, rejoicing not, appear.

This boy, then, suffering in the cedar-grove,
All rapturously, the uniting in his mind
Of these far-parted thoughts,—the boughs above,
And the priest's blessing o'er his head declined—

Is, in embyro beauteousness, one of that band,
Who, telling the sameness of far-parted things,
Plants through the universe, with magician hand,
A clue which makes us following universe-kings.

One of the seers and prophets who bid men pause
In their blind rushing, and awake to know
Fraternal essences and beauteous laws
In many a thing from which in scorn they go.

Yea, at his glance, sin's palaces may fall,
Men rise, and all their demon gods disown;
For knowledge of hidden resemblances is all
Needed to link mankind in happiness round Love's
    throne.

Studies of Resemblance and Consent.

[The eight poems which conclude this volume have all
appeared in print before,—all but the last two in the
author's lifetime. They are grouped here, as will
also be the poems to be printed for the first time
in the second volume, under the title of *Studies of
Resemblance and Consent*, in accordance with a design
of the author which, owing to circumstances detailed
more fully in the introductory portion of this book,
he was never able to complete.]

WHEN THE WORLD IS BURNING.*

(STANZAS FOR MUSIC.)

WHEN the world is burning,
Fired within, yet turning
    Round with face unscathed ;
Ere fierce flames, uprushing,
O'er all lands leap, crushing,
    Till earth fall, fire-swathed ;
Up amidst the meadows,
Gently through the shadows,
    Gentle flames will glide,
Small, and blue, and golden.
Though by bard beholden,
When in calm dreams folden,—-
    Calm his dreams will bide.

---

* Printed in *Ainsworth's Magazine*, January, 1845.

Where the dance is sweeping,
Through the greensward peeping,
  Shall the soft lights start ;
Laughing maids, unstaying,
Deeming it trick-playing,
High their robes upswaying,
  O'er the lights shall dart ;
And the woodland haunter
Shall not cease to saunter
  When, far down some glade,
Of the great world's burning
One soft flame upturning
Seems, to his discerning,
  Crocus in the shade.

My wife and child, come close to me,
The world to us is a stormy sea :
With your hands in mine, if your eyes but shine,
I care not how wild the storm may be.

For the fiercest wind that ever blew
Is nothing to me, so I shelter you ;
No warmth do I lack, for the howl at my back
Sings down to my heart, "Man bold and true !"

A pleasant sail, my child, my wife,
O'er a pleasant sea, to many is life ;
The wind blows warm, and they dread no storm,
And wherever they go, kind friends are rife.

But, wife and child, the love, the love
That lifteth us to the saints above,
Could only have grown where storms have blown
The truth and strength of the heart to prove."

* Printed in *The Critic*, May 31, 1845.

TACT IN KINDNESS.*

WHAT its sound is to the shower,
What its smoothness to the flower,
What its silence to the kiss,—
All this tact to kindness is.

Of the sound of the rain, of the feel of the flower,
　Now there is not a bard but would carol the praise ;
Then to tact, when subservient to kindness its power,
　May not I fitly give one of my humble lays ?
For though tact be a word that weds music not kindly,
　Let the sweet of its meaning make up for its sound ;
Without tact all kindness must go to work blindly,
　And inflame when it seeks to relieve the heart's
　　wound.

* Printed in the *Illuminated Magazine,* and in the *Illustrated Family Journal,* July 5, 1845.

Granted sometimes deception included in tact,
    And oftenest deception the handmaid of sin ;
Yet deception sometimes is by virtue enact,
    And some universal applauses shall win ;
Yea, though truth crowning glory of virtue is, still
    Sometimes 'tis a luxury the good must forego ;
Ask Trotty* who feign'd to have supp'd that starved
      Will
    Might eat the whole meal, yet without remorse go.

Oh ! seem when one serving, to be yourself served;
    Conceal not your blush when entirely bestowing ;
Expose, if you're woman, yourself all unnerved,
    When a lover's false hopes kindly all overthrowing;
Serve not on one absolute plan, as though tending
    Herds or flocks ; but each kindness effect in a way
To each weakness adapted, and so be commending
    That tact half whose goodness words fail to display.

      What its sound is to the shower,
      What its smoothness to the flower,
      What its silence to the kiss,—
      All this tact to kindness is.

    * The Trotty Veck of " The Chimes."

SEEKERS.*

Twice three years in this tomb she hath lain ;
      Speak low, speak low.
One like to her doth the earth yet contain ?
We have sought ever ; is the search vain ?
      Speak low.

Answer we nothing ? none have we found ?
      Weep not, weep not.
One like to her earth could but wound,
Sense with but wearying trammels bound ;—
      Weep not.

I would not meet one like to her !
      Start not, start not.

* Printed in *The Illuminated Magazine*, 1845.

Not with hope search I the world's strife and stir,
Ne'er at two shrines be I worshipper;—
    Start not.

Part we now from around her tomb,—
    Speak low, speak low.
East and west, through the world's gloom,
Seeking ever till here we come;—
    Speak low.

September **1845.**

THE MISANTHROPE'S CURE.*

One had counted every blow
Which the lofty deal the low,
Till his wretched soul could know
    Nought beside.

And to him earth seem'd a plain
Where each strove his good to gain
Through some other's loss or pain ;
    Evil all.

Common fate ! such watch will blind
Even a wise and learned mind
To the goodness in mankind
    Rooted deep.

For—be it well or be it ill—
To each man the universe will,
Like his own experience, still
    Ever loom.

* Printed in *The People's Journal*, November 28, 1846.

He grew sick with wrath and gloom;
And one day, to ask his doom,
In the leech's waiting-room
   Waited pale.

But a dame and maid coming in,
He from *them* his cure did win;
How, it were a heavy sin
   Ever to hide.

From the city's farthest side,
Through the city five miles wide,
Twice each week the dame here hied,
   Lone and old,

To be present while the maid,
Paying nought, sought the leech's aid;
Lest the maid's fair fame might fade,
   Hied she here.

Told this, to the dame he said,
"Five miles walk'd you with this maid?"
Said she, "For her ride I paid;
   She is ill."

"Then you are kin to her?" said he;
"No, oh no! but those that be
Would not do it, sir," answer'd she
      Softly still.

Ask'd he, "Could you both not ride?"
"Little, since my husband died,
Have I; she has nothing," replied
      Yet the dame.

Look'd he wondering in her face;
Heavenly shone its human grace;
And to him the world apace
      Heavenly shone.

As when in a wood a shower
Lights up every leaf and flower,
Was the universe in this hour
      Lit for him.

Oh let none learn good by stealth;
Tombing so earth's real wealth;
Thus regain'd its moral health
      This poor soul.

I BELIEVE.*

"Nature is not malignant like the gods of the people ; she is dreadfully imperfect, but has shown herself capable of improvement."—BARKER.

Every ship, except the ship we embark in,
        Gives us dreams
Of bright voyaging, beauteous lands afar, and
        Glorious streams ;
Every maiden, until she has consented,
        Angel seems.

Beautiful is nought, unless some foreground
        Grasp debar ;
All things flying attract us, and all charm till
        Gain'd they are ;
The hills are beautiful but because their summits
        Soar afar.

* Printed in *The Reasoner*, May 15, 1859.

What is the argument of thy discontent,
        Human soul?
Wilt thou, oh haggardest of coursers! ever
        Find fit goal?
Art thou a wild exception, or knoweth Nature
        Nothing whole?

Sometimes I dream the law of thy well-being
        Ceaseless change,
And while thy senses and affections bid thee
        Narrow range,
Thou, like a bird encaged and fetter'd, pinest
        Lost and strange.

But most I pondering deem that it may be
        That thy sight
To grasp the perfect 'neath Time's imperfections
        Hath no might,
Whilst only before the perfect canst thou expand to
        Fit delight.

And seems it then, whilst each fruit thou pursuest
        Turns to dust,
That, spite of all thy pride in thy pursuing,

'Twere more just
That thou hadst never been unto dead-sea apples
. Thus out-thrust.

Wait, blind-whirl'd Ixion of the flashing wheels,
Life and Death !
This thing is certain, that like ore good grows all
Ill beneath ;
Other than worshippers of dreams and scriptures
Live by faith.

Tombs many yet may rise for us, of lifetimes
Dark and brief ;
We may not see Time's victory, but it comes, and,
For our grief,
Endurance knows celestial consolations
Past belief.

Dissatisfaction accident is of Earth,
Not Earth's plan ;
Years come when even its name shall be a riddle
None may scan ;
Perchance even now his plumes outspreads the hour that
Ends the ban.

Roll on then, Earth, with all thy soaring mountains
         Pale as Ghosts !
Enchant, oh maids, and glory in enchanting
         Man's young hosts ;
Toward a new future will we make your victims
         Road sign-posts.

Mix pigments, study lines, **exalt us Nature**,
         Painters all,
Burn fire on all her altars ; and, though wearied,
         Never fall ;
What if 'twere come that she a Cleopatra
         Could not pall.

Hills, shake not off one torrent, nor grow pale thou,
         Golden Sun !
The music of the world thou light'st up hath not
         Yet begun.
Get ready, women ! fitly have ye not yet
         Once been won.

Nor shake thou mockingly thy dart, oh Death !
         Know, oh king !
We have made friends with Melancholy, and she

Thee will bring
Gently among us, yea to teach new music
Them that sing.

There is a heaven, though we to hope to pass there
May not dare ;
Where adoration shall for ever adore some
Perfect fair ;
And we can wait thee, Death, our eyes enfixed
Firmly there.

Jersey.

A WINTER HYMN TO THE SNOW.*

Come o'er the hills, and pass unto the wold,
And all things, as thou passest, in rest upfold,
  Nor all night long thy ministrations cease ;
Thou succourer of young corn, and of each seed
In plough'd land sown, or lost on rooted mead,
  And bringer everywhere of exceeding peace !

Beneath the long interminable frost
Earth's landscapes all their excellent force have lost,
  And stripp'd and abject each alike appears ;
Not now to adore can they exalt the soul,—
Panic, or anger, or unrest control,—
  Or aid the loosening of Affliction's tears.

* Printed in *The Athenæum*, September 14, 1878.

No more doth Desolateness lovely sit
Lone on the moor; no more around her flit
  From far high-travelling heaven the sailing shades;
The shrunk grass shivers feebly; reed and sedge,
By frozen marsh, by rivulet's iron edge,
  Bow, blent into the ice, mix'd stems and blades.

The mountains soar not, holding high in heaven
Their mighty kingdoms, but all downward driven
  Seem shrunken haggard ridges running low;
And all about stand drear upon the leas,
Like giant thorns, the frozen skeleton trees,
  Dead to the winds that ruining through them go.

The woodland rattles in the sudden gusts;
Frozen through frozen brakes the river thrusts
  His arm forth stiffly, like one slain and cold;
The glory from the horizon-line has fled;
One sullen formless gloom the skies are spread,
  And black the waters of the lakes are roll'd.

Come! Daughter fair of Sire the sternest, come,
And bring the world relief! to rivers numb
  Give garments, cover broadly the broad land;

All trees with thy resistless gentleness
Assume, and in thine own white vesture dress,
    And hush all nooks with thy persistings bland.

Come ! making rugged gorge and rocky height
Even more than fur of ermine soft and white,
    And cover up and silence roads and lanes ;
And, while the ravish'd wind sleeps hush'd and still,
Wreaths, little infancy with glee to fill,
    Upheap at doorways and at casement-panes.

Fancy's most potent pandar ! gentlest too :
Man, rising on the morn, the scene will view
    Thus, all transform'd, with no less sweet surprise
Than stirreth him to whose half-doubting sight
Sudden appears beloved friend, masqued bright
    In not less fair than unexpected guise.

And some will think the earth, in white robes drest,
Seems sinking fast in a great trance of rest,
    Beyond all further reach of wintry ill ;
And some will say it seems as though a ghost
Appear'd ; and thus, on fancy's seas far toss'd,
    With doubtful shadowy joys their spirits fill.

Thy task complete, if to the amazing scene
With Night should come, full-orb'd, Night's radiant
      Queen,
  How the whole race from out their homes will gaze !
Hard hearts will restless grow, and mean men sigh,
And wish they could be holier, and on high
  Some, whispering words of heaven, meek thanks
    will raise.

I, sweet celestial kisser ! from croft home-crown'd,
From ancient mead by stateliest trees girt round,
  From wilds where thou the earth lovest all alone,
Shall watch thee shower thy kisses, and all the hours
Rapt worship solemnize, and bless the Powers
  That let thy loveliness to my soul be known !

TO DEATH.*

I see thee in the churchyard, Death,
　　And fain would talk with thee,
While still I draw the young man's breath
　　And still with clear eyes see.

Thou wilt not make my spirit sink,
　　Thou dost not move my fear;
More sad more blest I often think
　　The mortal sojourner here.

Here where the symbols all of fair
　　With vileness mix'd we find;
Where knowledge soothes not, and where care
　　Haunts most the finest mind.

* Printed in the *Academy*, November 16, 1878.

'Tis thou who know'st if any knows
   Of life's wild maze the key ;
And if behind its marvellous shows
   Some Master moving be.

And haply of some farther life
   That shall this life adjust,
Or if we are men for threescore years,
   And then unconscious dust.

For this, oh Death, of thee I crave
   Some sign ; but not to pray
Against the inevitable grave
   Or self-contain'd decay.

Alas ! since first our fragile race
   Appear'd this earth upon,
Hast thou been question'd thus, and trace
   Of answer never won.

In vain the young from youth's delights,
   From lips whose kissing bloom
Bright chaos makes of days and nights,
   To thee defiant come.

In vain the old with trembling tread
  And trembling hands applies,
And strives to coax thy silence dread,
  And lifts beseeching eyes.

And vainly I desert my post
  In life's poor puppet game,
And seek thee where this silent host
  Of tombs thy power proclaim.

When midnight wraps the world in sleep,
  Or when the vanishing stars
And morn once more, new day to keep,
  Rolls back her golden bars.

In vain, in vain, but one reply
  In thy sad realm I find ;
Some fresh grave ever meets the eye,
  And mocks the unanswer'd mind.

June 10, 1860.

A WARNING.*

HE took his heart away from his fellows,
  And gave it to angels fair;
But the angels cannot commune with the human,
  Nor, if they could, would they dare.

Then took he back his heart from the angels,
  And over it long he mourn'd;
For he either could not or would not offer it
  Back to the race he scorn'd.

But all things die if utterly self-bound;
  And slowly this lone heart died:
And ever the Scorner is doom'd to wander,
  Meaner than all beside.

* Printed in *The Illuminated Magazine*, 1845.